PROVOCATION

USA TODAY BESTSELLING AUTHOR
T.K. LEIGH

PROVOCATION

Published by Carpe Per Diem, Inc

Edited by Kim Young, Kim's Editing Services

Cover Design: Cat Head Biscuit, Inc., Santa Clarita, CA

Cover assets:

© Pugavica88

Used under license from Deposit Photos.

BOOKS BY T.K. LEIGH

ROMANTIC SUSPENSE

The Temptation Series

Temptation

Persuasion

Provocation

Obsession

The Inferno Saga

Part One: Spark

Part Two: Smoke

Part Three: Flame

Part Four: Burn

CONTEMPORARY ROMANCE

The Redemption Duet

Commitment

Redemption

The Possession Duet

Possession

Atonement

The Dating Games Series

Dating Games

Wicked Games

Mind Games

Dangerous Games

Royal Games

Tangled Games

For more information on any of these titles and upcoming releases, please visit T.K.'s website:

www.tkleighauthor.com

PROLOGUE
(END OF PERSUASION)

Nick

Chains rattled against concrete in the long empty corridor as Domenic Jaskulski shuffled the best he could with the shackles around his ankles, two guards in front, two behind.

Nick could just barely make out the occasional, faint *buzz* of doors being opened and closed, but otherwise, it was relatively quiet in this area of the prison.

Or as quiet as anywhere in a prison could possibly be.

"You know the drill," one of the obtuse guards grunted in an unrefined, Southern accent that gave all people from this part of the country the reputation of being an inbred hillbilly.

Nick had zero patience for those who had no desire to better themselves. To educate themselves. It made him wild with rage.

But he wouldn't act on it.

It was important he not draw any attention to himself.

Otherwise, the plan to finally be reunited with his one true love would fall apart.

He couldn't have that.

"Would you be so kind as to remind me of the *drill* again, Officer?" Nick asked, his voice exuding superiority and class. "I don't believe I quite remember, as I've only been doing this *very* thing every week for the past several years."

"Enough with the snotty remarks, jackass."

The officer opened the door, practically pushing Nick into the room, causing him to stumble slightly. Grabbing his elbow, he dragged him toward the table where a man dressed in black sat, patiently waiting for their weekly spiritual advisement.

"But I do so enjoy our banter. I find our conversations quite...invigorating. Intellectually stimulating. Why, just last week, I was surprised to learn you knew the proper use of regardless, instead of using *irregardless*. I'll be honest. Hearing some of your brethren utter that abomination makes me just...murderous."

"Shut it, asswipe," the officer ordered, all but shoving

him onto the cold, metal chair. "Or I'll revoke your visitation privileges for the next month, *irregardless* of whether it's a clergy visit."

The officer retrieved a key from his belt, forcing Nick's hands on the table. With rough motions, he secured the cuffs to the bar in the center, shot Nick a glare, then retreated from the stark, cold room.

Unlike the other visitation rooms, there were no windows. No cameras. Nothing.

There couldn't be. It wasn't allowed when inmates met with their lawyers or spiritual advisors. It was truly the only place one could conduct any conversation in private.

And, for these conversations, privacy was essential.

Once the heavy door slammed shut, the *buzz* indicating it was locked, Nick slowly lifted his eyes to the young man sitting across the table, a leather-bound bible in front of him.

He pushed it toward Nick, who opened it to a book in *The Old Testament. Leviticus,* to be precise. When his eyes fell on a photo, his heart skipped a beat, a slow smile curving on his lips at the woman in the image.

Beautiful.

Naked.

Dead.

"Forgive me, Father," Nick began, slowly raising his

gaze to meet a pair of clear, blue eyes, "for I believe *you* have sinned."

The visitor's lips twisted up in the corners, his devious grin nearly identical to Nick's.

"You know what they say. Like father, like son."

CHAPTER ONE

Lachlan

W as this what happiness felt like?

Considering it had been years since I'd experienced anything remotely close to it, I wasn't sure.

But as my eyes slowly opened, the sun streaming into the bedroom of my house in the Chastain Park neighborhood of Atlanta illuminating Julia's naked, slumbering form, I couldn't remember ever being so at peace. My heart feeling so full.

We'd only been back on the mainland for ten days, so we were still in the honeymoon stage. With her daughter away at camp, Julia was able to spend every free minute at my house. Couple that with the All-Star

Game being in Atlanta, along with a stretch of home games, it was as if nothing had changed.

Unfortunately, that all ended today.

In a few hours, I'd head to D.C. for a series of away games. And Julia would pick up her daughter from camp.

This new dynamic would certainly be an adjustment. I wasn't going to worry about it, though. I had to trust it would all work out. That there was a reason our paths crossed in Hawaii.

This woman was my absolution. My redemption.

And in my soul, I felt I was hers.

"I can hear you thinking."

Julia's sleep-filled voice cut through the silence.

A low chuckle rumbled from my chest as I hooked my arm around her waist, pulling her body back against mine.

"You can *hear* me thinking?" I left a trail of kisses along her shoulder blade, focusing my attention on that spot where her neck met her shoulders, fully aware how much it drove her wild when I kissed her there.

"Always." The word came out as a moan.

"Then what am I thinking?"

"I don't know *what* you're thinking. Just that you are."

I circled my hips against her. "How about now?"

Her laughter filled the room. It should have seemed

strange to hear such an endearing sound in a house that had never been home to anything resembling happiness.

But with Julia, it felt right.

"Okay. *Now* I know exactly what you're thinking." She wiggled against me, hardening my erection even more.

"You little tease." I nipped at her neck.

She turned to face me, our eyes meeting. As I stared into those brilliant, green pools, my heart brimmed with an emotion I couldn't even begin to understand.

For the past several weeks, I kept thinking I'd wake up and discover everything had been nothing more than a dream. That I'd imagined Julia.

But if this were a dream, I didn't care. I didn't need to live in the real world. I'd happily reside in this place of fantasies, as long as Julia remained here with me.

"I thought you liked it when I teased you." She ran her fingers through my hair, nails digging into my scalp, setting me on fire.

"I don't just like it." I pushed her onto her back and hovered over her, smoothing a few auburn waves behind her ear. "I bloody love it. Crave it. Am desperate for it." I lowered my mouth to hers. "I'm so damn desperate for you."

"Then have me."

With a needy groan, I positioned myself at her

entrance before easing inside her. She arched her back, mouth opening in bliss.

It didn't matter how many times we'd done this over the past few weeks. Every time felt different. A new way to experience her. A new way to cherish her.

I grabbed her wrists in my hands, pinning her arms over her head as I slowly and sensually rocked my hips against her.

"You're a dream, love. A fucking perfect dream come true." I covered her mouth with mine, swallowing her moans as I showed her how much I needed her in my life.

I wasn't a fool, though.

We may have left Hawaii, but we were still in the clouds. Still enclosed in the bubble we'd constructed around ourselves during what was only supposed to be one week together.

But today, we had to return to earth. Had to face reality.

I had to believe everything would be okay. That despite the obstacles ahead, we'd survive.

Like *Eme* said... It was just noise.

So instead of worrying about something I had little control over, I focused on this place where Julia and I did connect.

As I watched her body writhe beneath mine seconds

before I succumbed to my own bliss, I knew this was where I was meant to be.

With this woman.

In her life.

And hopefully in her heart.

CHAPTER TWO

Julia

The aroma of onions and peppers surrounded me as I stirred the potato mixture, taking advantage of Lachlan's gourmet kitchen.

For a man who paid someone to prepare all his meals, he had an incredible setup.

Then again, this house was a dream. I practically had to pick my jaw up off the ground when I first pulled up to it.

I grew up in a wealthy family. The daughter of a notable architect. Now the sister of one.

But Lachlan's house was on a completely different level. Maybe it was because he was so young that it seemed much more impressive. It served as a stark reminder of exactly who he was — one of the highest paid pitchers in the history of baseball.

I considered myself successful. But my success paled compared to Lachlan's. And this house was evidence of everything he'd achieved in such a short time.

Despite all of that, it lacked...personality. Sure, the back yard boasted a baseball diamond and batting cage. Not to mention a massive, detached garage filled with classic cars, another love of his I'd recently learned about.

Other than that, though, this could have passed as one of my brother's model homes. Gorgeous. Glamourous. Impersonal.

Maybe I'd been a mom for so long that I'd grown accustomed to a chaotic home and life. Nearly every surface of my house was covered with photos of Imogene throughout the years. Her first step. First lost tooth. First day of school.

Why didn't Lachlan have any photos of his family?

It seemed odd, considering how close he claimed to be with his sister.

I tried not to fixate on it. Figured there had to be some logical reason behind it. Told myself not everyone liked to clutter their homes with photos and mementos.

Perhaps with his hectic schedule and the fact all sorts of people had access to his house — housekeeper, groundskeeper, pool cleaner, car detailer, chef — he didn't want to leave personal photos lying around for fear someone might share them.

At least that was what I tried to convince myself as I gave the potatoes another stir, then opened the oven to check on the frittata.

Typically, Lachlan liked making breakfast for me. But since he had to leave town today for a stretch of away games, he was the one who needed to hop into the shower and pack. So I offered to make him a breakfast filled with all the stuff he needed to eat for peak performance. Tons of carbs with some lean protein and healthy fats thrown in for good measure.

Another reason I hated him.

If I so much as looked at a morsel of pasta, I gained weight. However, when Lachlan polished off huge plates of food, I swore a few more ripples of muscle sprouted on his already sculpted body.

"Whatever you're making smells absolutely incredible."

I straightened from the oven, skillet in hand, and looked Lachlan's way, inhaling a sharp breath as he entered the kitchen.

Over the course of our short relationship, I'd seen this man dressed in a variety ways.

And *un*dressed in a variety of ways, too.

But the sight of Lachlan in a crisp, perfectly molded, navy blue suit was something else altogether.

"God bless Australia," I murmured, certain a bit of drool escaped my mouth. "And the team rule requiring you to wear a suit during travel."

Lachlan's laughter echoed against the high ceilings. "I take it you don't hate this look on me."

"Hate it?" I set the skillet on the stove and wiped my hands on a kitchen towel. Then I sauntered up to him, feeling woefully underdressed in my shorts and t-shirt. Hell, I wasn't even wearing a bra or underwear. Lachlan's voracious sexual appetite rendered them mostly useless anyway.

Hell, *my* voracious sexual appetite did, too.

Placing my hands on the lapels of his jacket, I hoisted myself onto my toes, curving toward him, my mouth practically watering with the promise of his kiss.

"Seeing you like this makes me want to climb on top of you." I grabbed his tie and pulled him toward me, his lips a breath from mine.

"That can be arranged, love. That can most certainly be arranged."

He crushed his mouth to mine, wrapping an arm around my body, tugging me against him. I closed my eyes, savoring in everything this man had become to me. I didn't think I'd ever crave a man with the kind of intensity I had for Lachlan. Didn't think it was possible.

But Lachlan proved all my preconceived notions wrong.

He'd become such a big part of my life in only a few weeks. I thought of him every waking hour. Hell, there were times he'd even managed to find his way into my dreams. Maybe this was the fun phase of a relationship I'd always heard people talk about. That time when you couldn't get enough of each other. When you wanted to spend every possible minute together.

I'd never experienced something like this. I'd lived most of my life on the defensive, waiting for it all to fall apart.

But with Lachlan, I refused to assume that was going to happen. Refused to continue to live in survival mode.

For once, I was going to allow myself to be happy without fear of when the bottom would drop.

"If you don't stop kissing me, your breakfast will get cold," I warned, pushing against him and returning to the stove.

Feeling Lachlan's stare on me, I looked in his direction, my pulse increasing at the heat in his gaze as he stalked toward me.

"I'll gladly suffer those consequences if it means I can have you one more time." He stopped behind me, a hand going to my hip, fingers grazing the skin.

"But your car will be here soon."

When his unshaven jawline scratched against my neck, it took every ounce of resolve I possessed to not spread my legs so I could feel him one last time before he left.

"Are you turning me down, Julia?"

"Never. But someone has to be the responsible one. You don't want to get oil spotted, do you?"

He buried his head in my neck. Then he groaned, releasing his hold. "I guess you're right."

"I usually am." I glanced behind me and winked before returning my attention to the skillet. When Lachlan smacked my ass, I yelped and flung my gaze to his. My heart fluttered at the playful smirk tugging on that sinful mouth.

"Sorry, love." He pressed a kiss to my neck. "Couldn't resist." He cupped my backside. "I bloody love this arse." After nipping my skin, he pulled back, making his way toward his gourmet espresso machine.

I faced forward, cutting through the frittata and plating two portions, adding potatoes to both. I couldn't help but smile at how normal and easy things were with Lachlan. It almost seemed too good to be true. I refused to go down that road, though. Wasn't going to sabotage this because I wasn't used to good things happening to me. After everything I'd been through, I deserved to be happy.

And there was no doubt. Lachlan made me deliriously happy.

Once I finished, I scooted around to the other side of

the massive island and set the dishes down. Always the gentleman, Lachlan pulled out a barstool, helping me into it before sitting beside me.

"Thanks for this," he said as he placed a napkin across his lap.

"I figured it was my turn to finally make you breakfast, since that seems to have become your thing."

"I like cooking for you. I can't make much, but I can handle eggs." He looked at his plate. "I doubt I'll ever be able to make something like this, though." He grabbed his fork and sliced into the frittata. When he took a bite, he moaned in appreciation, chewing for a few minutes before swallowing. "Correction. I *know* I won't be able to make something like this. It's bloody delicious, Julia."

I shrugged. "It's just eggs, spinach, and mushrooms. Oh, and feta cheese. If you ask me, feta makes everything better."

"Well, it's fantastic. A man could get used to this."

I held his gaze. "So could a woman."

"Good." He placed a chaste kiss on my cheek before digging back into his breakfast.

After a moment, he looked at me. "Are you nervous about today?"

"A little," I answered around a bite of potatoes. "I'm excited to see Imogene after three weeks. But that also means telling her everything that's happened. And, honestly, I'm not quite sure what I'm going to tell her."

"What do you mean?" He lowered his voice. "You're not having second thoughts about this, are you?"

I darted my wide eyes to his. "What?! Of course not. I just..." I blew out a breath. "I'm going to tell her about you. About us. But teenagers are a tough breed. Especially girls. This could be difficult for her. It's a lot of change all at once. Not only is she about to learn her mom's dating someone again after refusing to even entertain the notion for years, but I have to tell her that person is thirteen years younger...and is her favorite player from her favorite team. There's no telling how she'll handle that."

"I may not know much about her, apart from the bits you've shared with me, but she sounds like a pretty level-headed kid."

"Kid..." I laughed to myself over the irony, considering the age difference between Lachlan and Imogene was the same as it was between him and me.

"Whatever..." He waved me off, shoveling more food into his mouth, his breakfast almost gone. Once he swallowed and washed it down with a sip of espresso, he continued. "It doesn't matter. All that does is whatever obstacles we face going forward, we face them together." He grasped my hand, squeezing. "Okay?"

"Okay."

"Okay," he repeated, lips brushing mine. But instead

of pulling back, he coaxed my mouth open, a renewed hunger filling me when his tongue touched mine.

How was it possible for me to crave this man as much as I did? By now, I expected I wouldn't be so desperate for him every minute of every day. But I still was. Which was going to make the next few days excruciatingly painful.

When the sound of the doorbell cut through, Lachlan groaned.

"Goddammit," he hissed, yet not making any move to pull back.

"Duty calls."

He hesitated, then reluctantly pulled away and stood. I did the same, about to grab our plates to clean up. But before I could, his arm looped around my waist, yanking my body against his.

"I've never wanted to stay here as badly as I do now. I normally look forward to road games. Not anymore." He framed my face in his hands. "Not if it means being away from you."

"But just think how amazing your first night back home will be." I waggled my brows. "We'll have four days' worth of catching up to do."

"I like the sound of that."

I draped my arms over his shoulders, toying with a few tendrils of his dark hair. "As do I." Tilting my head back, my lips sought out his.

I breathed into him, Lachlan's hold on me tightening as his tongue tangled with mine. He moved a hand from my face, roaming down the curve of my frame. Lifting my t-shirt, his fingers traced my stomach before brushing against the swell of my breast.

My core clenched, every inch of my body throbbing with a yearning only he could satisfy.

The doorbell rang again.

Lachlan tore his lips from mine. "Bloody hell. One second."

He stormed toward the foyer, pausing to adjust himself before opening the door. "I just need five more minutes to finish eating," he told the man in a dark suit standing outside.

"Yes, sir. Traffic is light, so that won't be a problem."

"Thanks, mate." Lachlan closed the door and stalked back toward me.

I glanced at his plate, which he'd licked clean. "Finish eating?" I crossed my arms in front of my chest. "Looks like you're finished to me."

With a sly smirk, he shrugged off his jacket and loosened his tie, his carnal look sending a thrill through me.

"Not quite."

Before I could respond, he reached for my shorts and yanked them down my legs. Grabbing my hips, he lifted me onto the kitchen island.

As he slid his hands up my thighs, my pulse skyrocketed.

"One more for the road, beautiful." Lowering himself between my legs, he flicked his tongue against my clit.

I closed my eyes, running my fingers through his hair as I moved with the rhythm he set.

"I think I'm really going to like road games."

CHAPTER THREE

Julia

"She lives," Wes joked when he let himself into my house later that morning.

"Of course I live," I shot back, ignoring the insinuation in his remark as I finished packing snacks for our drive. It reminded me of the trips we took to the beach as teenagers. Wes would always drive. I'd always bring the snacks.

"Pretty sure this is the longest you've gone without stopping by my house, especially considering Imogene's been out of town. In the past, you've practically lived at my place whenever she was at camp. Hell, I even asked if you wanted to come down to Meemaw and Gampy's old lake house last weekend, but you said you couldn't."

I shrugged. "I've been busy."

"Yeah." He leaned against the island and waggled his brows. "Getting busy."

"Wes!" I playfully punched his arm. "What are you? Twelve?"

"No. I'm just glad you're finally dating again. And that you're happy."

He left a kiss on my temple before pulling back, meeting my gaze.

"All joking aside, how's it going? Is he treating you well? Because, I swear to God, I don't care if he's bigger than me, stronger than me, and can probably kill me with his bare hands. If he so much as even thinks about hurting you, I—"

I placed a hand on his arm. "He's the perfect gentleman, Wes," I assured him. "Well, maybe not a *complete* gentleman." I gave him a sly smile. "But he's perfect. It's been...perfect."

"Good."

He smiled, then cleared his throat.

It was an innocent sound, but being as close as we were, having the ability to pick up on each other's moods, I heard a hint of uncertainty.

"What's wrong?" I asked.

He didn't immediately respond. Finally, he sighed. "Agent Curran called right before I left to come here."

My shoulders fell. "Oh."

I knew we'd have to face reality at some point. Get answers about what was going on. Try to figure out if Nick were still somehow involved in taking women's lives, even from behind bars.

"Did he find something?"

"He wouldn't say. Asked if we were available to meet with him this weekend."

"This weekend? Why can't we just go to his office during the week?"

With Lachlan gone until Monday night, I'd planned to spend the next few days with Imogene. Go to the spa. Get mani-pedis. Take her shopping for the start of school in a few weeks. Stay up late watching movies. Appreciate what precious little time I could get with my daughter now that she was a teenager and her friends were her life.

"I don't know. All I do know is that he insisted we talk as soon as possible."

I didn't like the sound of that. Part of me wanted to remain blissfully ignorant of whatever was going on. But I did that during my marriage, and it cost several women their lives.

"Okay. Set it up for whenever it's convenient for you."

"Will do."

I chewed on my bottom lip. "What do *you* think is going on, Wes? Are you worried?"

He ran his hands through his dark hair that had a few flecks of gray in it, giving me a sideways glance. Then he pushed out a long breath.

"Yes, I'm worried. For Londyn. For Imogene. For Eli. For my unborn daughter. But mostly, I'm worried for you, Jules. I don't think 'worried' is the right word here, though. It's more..." He shook his head, then brought his gaze back to mine. "It's more like I am fucking terrified what this could all mean."

I hated the thought he'd probably lost sleep over this since he'd learned the possible connection between the "gifts" I'd received and more bodies.

"Wes...," I began in a soothing voice.

He held up his hand, stopping me before I made him any false promises. "I understand that we don't know anything for certain, and I am trying to not jump to any conclusions here. But I'm also trying to think rationally. Trying to take into account everything we know about Nick. Luckily, we have the advantage of knowing a lot more about him than most people. Which is why I don't think he's stopped obsessing over you, Julia. Not for a goddamn second." He stepped closer, dropping his voice. "I heard what he told you that day."

I swallowed hard. "What day?" I asked, although I feared I already knew the answer.

"At the hospital after he attacked you and you stabbed him. When you went to go see him one last time before he was officially taken into police custody. I was right outside. I heard him, Julia." He leaned toward me, the muscles in his jaw tight. "Heard his threat. Because that's exactly what it was. Not some sweet repetition of his vow to love you until he took his final breath. 'Till death do us part'?"

His words came out choked, every inch of him trembling with a mixture of anger and apprehension.

"That was a threat. Or, more accurately, a promise. *That's* why I've been so adamant about you pushing Agent Curran to get more information about where this jewelry could be coming from. Because I know a life sentence in prison isn't going to stop Nick. He'll find a way to get to you." He grabbed my hand in his. "I'm petrified he already has."

"Wes..." I wrapped my arms around him, trying to offer some sort of comfort. I'd been so concerned about how this could potentially affect me that I hadn't even stopped to consider how Wes was handling it. "It'll be okay. I'm okay. It won't be like before. I'm stronger than I was back then." I pulled back and met his eyes. "Thanks to you."

"Nah. That's all you. You're a badass, Julia Blaire. I wouldn't want to cross you. Before Londyn got pregnant, I watched you two box together. You've got a mean right hook."

"I appreciate your vote of confidence." I winked,

trying to cut through the tension. "And you never know. All this worrying could be for nothing. That could be what Agent Curran wants to tell us. That the jewelry I've received aren't the originals. That it *is* the work of a true crime fanatic, like he initially thought."

"Do you really believe that?"

Pinching my lips into a tight line, I subtly shook my head. "No, I don't."

He pulled me into his arms once more. "Neither do I."

CHAPTER FOUR

Julia

A s if by unspoken agreement, neither Wes nor I brought up Agent Curran or my ex-husband during the two-hour drive north. Instead, our conversation focused on my time in Hawaii, Lachlan, and the preparations he and Londyn had started making prior to welcoming baby number two in a few months.

I had to swallow down the hint of jealousy that built inside me at the reminder of my older brother having another baby this late in the game. At least for him. Then again, Londyn *was* still in her thirties. Regardless, a part of me stirred with emotion over the fact he and Londyn were able to have another baby. Unfortunately, that wasn't an option for me.

Or Lachlan.

Did he realize that?

Sure, I'd told him I couldn't get pregnant, which had allowed us to dispense with condoms. But I didn't go into any specific details.

Did he understand that it wasn't simply because I was on the pill or had some sort of IUD that could be easily removed? That I'd done something more permanent?

Did he even want kids?

Would this be a dealbreaker?

There were so many things I didn't know about him. So many important conversations we'd never touched on. Granted, it was still early in our relationship. But were we setting ourselves up for failure by not discussing all these things before jumping into...whatever this was?

"Earth to Julia...," Wes sang, pulling me out of my increasingly unsettled thoughts.

I snapped back to the present, realizing Wes' Range Rover had not only come to a stop, but was parked in the dirt lot in front of the large, log cabin-style building that served as the community hall for the summer camp Imogene had attended the past six years.

"Sorry. Guess I was daydreaming." I flashed Wes a smile, then unhooked my seat belt and opened the passenger door.

"About Lachlan?" he teased as he jumped out of the car, walking around to join me.

"Something like that," I answered, my voice lacking any sort of enthusiasm.

"Hey." Wes touched my arm, gently turning me to face him. "Are you okay?" He dropped his voice. "I'm sorry for what I said back at the house. I didn't mean to worry you. I just—"

"It's okay. I'm glad you did. I asked for your honesty, and that's what you gave me," I assured him, not wanting to tell him what I was really thinking about. He'd think I was crazy for going there when Lachlan and I hadn't even been together a month. What couple discussed kids so soon?

Then again, we weren't most couples.

"Let's stop worrying about it now." I smiled. "For one day, let's pretend there's no Agent Curran. No Nick. No stupid necklaces. Or bracelets. Or anything else. We're just a normal family living a normal life."

"Sounds like a plan to me." He draped his arm over my shoulders and led me toward the community hall.

After we checked in, we were each given a visitor's badge and allowed into the camp, which consisted of hundreds of acres of nothing but trees, lakes, and mountains.

Initially, I hated the idea of sending Imogene so far away for three weeks every summer. But my therapist suggested it as a way for me to cope with my separation anxiety, at least when it came to my daughter.

In the aftermath of Nick's arrest, I tended to smother her, more so than normal. Anytime I heard so much as a floorboard creak in the house, I rushed to check on her, make sure she was okay. Hell, some nights I even crawled into bed with her, so damn terrified Nick would get revenge by having Imogene kidnapped.

It was what he did during our marriage, constantly controlling and manipulating me to do what he wanted by threatening to take Imogene from me. He may have never come right out and said the words. He didn't have to. He showed me with his actions. With the stupid games he played.

So the thought of my daughter being hundreds of miles away where anything could happen nearly killed me. But my therapist assured me it was crucial for Imogene's emotional development.

And mine.

"Mama!"

At the sound of the familiar voice, I darted my eyes toward the lake, easily spotting Imogene amongst the sea of teenagers and adolescents, all wearing the same t-shirt with the camp logo on it.

"Imogene," I exhaled, as if a weight had suddenly lifted. That was what it felt like when I gazed upon my beautiful little girl, even if she weren't so little anymore.

She certainly didn't get her height from me, considering she already had a few inches on me, even at the age of fourteen.

But I refused to think about whom she *did* get her height from.

Nick no longer had any place in our lives.

Imogene touched her little cousin's shoulder, then pointed toward us. Eli spun around, a huge smile on his face, and sprinted toward Wes, jumping into his arms.

The first time I picked up Imogene from camp, she did the same. While she may not run toward me like she once did, not wanting to appear as if she missed her mom in front of her friends, her steps were still a bit quicker than normal, bordering on a jog. And when she wrapped her arms around me, her hug was just as tight as when she was a little girl.

"Hey, baby." I squeezed her to me, inhaling her scent. Fresh air. Powder. And something unique to my little girl. "I missed you."

"I missed you, too, Mama." She pulled back, her dark eyes studying my face. "How was Hawaii? Looks like you got some sun."

"That I did," I answered, sensing Wes' amused stare on me. "I'll tell you all about it when we get home."

"Can't wait." She gave me a smile before looking over my shoulder. "Hiya, Uncle Wes."

"Hey, peanut." He lowered Eli to his feet, then pulled her in for a tight squeeze.

"How did you like camp, Eli?" I crouched to my nephew's level. "Did you do anything exciting?"

"I learned to shoot a bow and arrow." His brown eyes lit up with the enthusiasm of a six-year-old little boy. "And I rode a horse. And paddled a canoe. And during the soccer clinic, I scored a goal against Mo!"

"Is that right?" Standing, I glanced in Imogene's direction.

"He's a natural." She shrugged, then winked.

I smiled, knowing Imogene let him score against her. She was normally a wall out on the field, barely anything ever getting past her. But the counselors here didn't focus on winning. Instead, it was all about instilling confidence in each kid, teaching them how to work as a team, regardless of whether they won or lost.

It brought to mind Lachlan's Little League in Hawaii. How passionate he was about instilling the same thing in every kid who walked onto the baseball diamond bearing his last name.

And like baseball changed those kids' lives, this camp changed Imogene's.

"Have you both said your goodbyes?" Wes looked between Eli and Imogene. "We've got a bit of a drive home, so we probably should get going."

"I just need one second." Imogene hoisted herself onto her toes and looked over dozens of kids and parents.

When someone called her name, her gaze darted toward the right, a blush covering her cheeks as a tall, lanky, dark-haired teenager jogged our way.

"Hey, Mo," he said, wearing a smile I would have easily swooned over when I was Imogene's age.

"Hey, Roman," she replied, pushing a few of her blonde waves behind her ear.

"Hey, Roman," I repeated, earning me a death glare from my daughter.

Roman turned his attention to me and cleared his throat. "Mrs. Prescott... Ma'am... Nice to meet you. I'm Roman Dean. I go to school with Imogene."

"So I've heard," I responded, ignoring the fact he'd called me *Mrs.* Prescott, then ma'am. After all, he *was* born and raised in the South, where referring to everyone as "sir" or "ma'am" was ingrained in all of us since birth. But being called ma'am mere days after celebrating my fortieth birthday felt different than prior years.

Still, I shrugged it off, taking it for what it was... A young teen who was interested in my daughter trying to be polite.

"She mentioned you were in Hawaii. Did you have a good time?"

"I did. Thank you for asking." I looked from Roman

to Imogene. "And I trust you two had a good time at camp? Imogene mentioned you both helped out in the soccer clinic?"

"Sure did." He beamed at Imogene, his eyes lighting up.

The way he looked at her was incredibly sweet. Exactly how I'd hoped a boy would look at her one day. Not like she was merely a piece of property.

"She's a great player."

Imogene grinned shyly, her fair skin not able to mask her growing blush.

"Well, it's a pleasure to meet you, Roman."

"You, too, Mrs. Prescott."

I smiled at him, then looked at Imogene. "You can take a few minutes to say goodbye."

"Thanks, Mama."

I gave them space, fully aware of how fragile teenagers could be about this kind of thing. Especially girls.

"Did you know about this?" Wes asked when I sidled up next to him.

"Know about what?"

"Imogene and that kid. Is that a thing?"

"His name is Roman. And I think it might be."

"And you're okay with it?"

"They go to school together. He's a preacher's kid." I snorted out a laugh. "Honestly, I'm more concerned

she'll make me go to church so she can see him. Damn
building will go up in flames."

I expected Wes to chuckle in agreement. Instead, he
stared at me, eyes wide. "Wow."

"Why are you so surprised at that? You know my
feelings on organized religion. I—"

"No. Not that. I'm talking about you being okay with
Imogene dating."

"She's fourteen. I can't keep her locked up
forever."

"Hmm..."

"What?"

"Nothing."

"No, Wes. You *hmm*-ed. You only do that when
keeping something from me."

"I was just thinking that it appears someone's had a
positive influence on you."

I furrowed my brows. "What do you mean?"

"If this happened a few months ago...hell, a few
weeks ago...you probably would have quickly ushered
Imogene out of here so she couldn't even entertain the
notion of talking to a boy. You're much more...relaxed."
He leaned closer, dropping his voice to a whisper.
"Guess you finally found someone to help take the edge
off."

"Weston James Bradford!" I retorted, playfully
smacking him in the stomach. But I couldn't stop the

smile that tugged on my lips at the memory of just how great Lachlan was at helping take the edge off.

I looked back at Imogene at the precise moment Roman whispered something into her ear. I could practically feel the butterflies fluttering in her stomach. It reminded me of the way I felt that first time Lachlan leaned toward me and whispered something into my ear.

Hell, it reminded me of the butterflies he *still* gave me.

"Mo-Mo has a boyfriend," Eli teased when Imogene jogged back toward us.

She rolled her eyes, exuding all the attitude of a teenage girl. "No, I don't."

"Then what was that?" Wes inquired, smirking.

"Nothing," she responded with a dismissive shrug. "He just asked if he could call me later tonight."

Her cell chimed from the back pocket of her shorts. She yanked it out. I didn't even need to peek at the screen to know who'd texted. Based on her wide grin and the pink hue of her cheeks, it was obvious it was from Roman. She giggled, glancing over her shoulder, biting her lower lip as he waved.

It was official. I wasn't ready for this.

But I doubted Imogene would be ready for my big news, either.

CHAPTER FIVE

Unknown

"Good evening, sir," a petite blonde said with a cordial smile as the man approached the concierge desk of the upscale hotel. "How can I be of service to you this evening?"

He glanced at the name tag attached to her gray suit jacket, then lifted his eyes to meet hers. "Hello, Katherine. Such a beautiful name. One you don't hear all that often these days."

The blonde's smile wavered, her fingers grasping her necklace, briefly toying with the pink, teardrop-shaped pearl. Her reaction only served to increase the man's curiosity.

"Th-thank you, sir," Katherine replied, her expression brightening once more. "What can I help you with this evening? Do you need assistance with dinner reservations? Sightseeing tours? Perhaps theater tickets?"

He studied the woman for a beat, observing her as she pushed a tendril of hair behind her ear, a blush blooming on her cheeks. She truly was beautiful. Flawless, creamy skin. Pink lips that weren't too thin or too full. Small, button nose. And innocent, blue eyes, making him think the world hadn't jaded her just yet.

"Actually..." He sat in one of the armchairs opposite the ornate, wooden desk, a smile curving his mouth. "I'd hoped to get a recommendation for dinner. I'm not too familiar with the area. Where do *you* like to eat?"

"I'm sure your preferences are much more sophisticated than mine." Pushing that same lock of hair behind her ear yet again, she chewed on her bottom lip.

It took every ounce of resolve he possessed to resist the temptation to ask if he could chew on her bottom lip, too.

That wasn't what tonight was about.

No. Tonight was simply a...reconnaissance mission. See if she fit the role he needed her to play.

If she did, he'd taste those lips soon enough.

"What makes you say that?"

"Look at you." She laughed nervously.

"What about me?"

He relaxed into the chair, resting his calf on his opposite knee, taking care to remember every detail about her. From the way she repeatedly licked her lips, to the sweet lilt in her voice, to the way she wouldn't look him directly in the eye.

God, she was perfect.

She gave him a knowing look, then leaned across the desk. As she did, he caught a whiff of her perfume. Powder. Rose water. Perhaps a hint of peppermint. She dropped her voice to barely louder than a whisper.

"Since you can afford a room at this hotel, where one night is about one week of my pay, your tastes are a bit more...refined than mine."

"Just because I can afford the more expensive things doesn't mean that's *all* I want out of life. You know what they say, don't you?" He brushed his thumb along his lower lip.

"What's that?"

He inched closer, still cognizant to keep a respectful amount of space between them. He couldn't raise any eyebrows. Couldn't make a mark. Couldn't have anyone remember him.

Except Katherine.

He most certainly wanted her to remember him.

Think of him.

Crave him.

Just like he craved her.

"Variety is the spice of life." He lingered for a moment before pulling back.

"So, give me some variety. I'm in town on business. Every night this week, I'm stuck in meetings at pretentious restaurants with white-gloved waitstaff and a wine list longer than Webster's Dictionary. Give me somewhere fun. Somewhere the drinks are strong and the food abundant. Give me something real."

"Something real…," she mused.

"Precisely."

She toyed with her necklace once more, most likely more out of habit than a conscious decision. Then she lifted her gaze to his.

For the first time, she peered directly into his eyes.

He was momentarily speechless at the vitality within, the blue hue so light it almost appeared gray.

"Okay. If you want something real, I have the perfect spot."

Grabbing a pen, she jotted something down on a small piece of hotel stationery, then ripped it off. When she stood, he did the same, taking the paper from her.

"The Joint?" he read.

"It might not look like much from the outside, but it will blow your mind. Best Southern cooking you'll find this side of the Mason-Dixon. And the best Old Fashioned, too." She winked. "If you're into that kind of thing."

"Sounds like exactly what I'm looking for." He smiled, his gaze sweeping over her slender frame one last time. "Thank you."

He turned, making his way across the ornate lobby, shoes echoing against the marble tile. Then he paused, glancing over his shoulder.

"And Katherine?"

She tore her eyes away from the computer on her desk, meeting his stare once more. "Yes?"

His lips curled into a sly grin. "That's a beautiful necklace."

CHAPTER SIX

Julia

"How was it to finally shower in your own bathroom?" I asked when Imogene walked into the kitchen.

"Transcendental," she exhaled. "Life changing."

I chuckled at her occasional flair for the dramatics.

"Don't get me wrong." She hoisted herself onto the barstool on the opposite side of the island.

The sight of her back where she belonged warmed my heart. It was like a missing piece of my life had been returned to its rightful place.

"I love camp, but it's nice to have my own space again after sharing a cabin with five other girls." She snorted and grabbed the bottle of water I'd set out for her. "One bathroom for five girls? Not exactly optimal conditions."

"I can imagine," I offered as I finished slicing the pepperoni stromboli I'd made. After arranging it on a serving tray, I set it on the island beside the plate of mushroom canapés she loved.

As Imogene scanned the small feast I'd prepared, her smile fell, eyes filled with concern.

"What happened?"

"What do you mean?"

She gestured in front of her. "Mushroom canapés. Pepperoni stromboli. French onion soup. Smothered chicken. All my favorite foods. There's definitely something going on." Her expression paled, trepidation covering her as she dropped her voice. "Is it something to do with...*him*?"

"No! Absolutely not!" I answered quickly, wanting to quash any hint of unease when it came to Nick.

"Are you sure? Because if he did something, you can tell me. You don't have to protect me from him. I'm not a little kid anymore. I can handle it."

I rushed over and pressed a hand to her cheek. "I know you can, baby."

At one time, whenever I looked into Imogene's dark eyes, I saw Nick, the similarity striking.

But as the years passed and she learned the truth about the man who held us prisoner in our lives for too long, I no longer saw Nick in any of her features. She grew into being her own person, completely independent from that monster.

In fact, at only seven, she'd handled the truth better than I expected.

Or maybe she was like me and had sensed something off about her father long before his crimes were revealed.

Long before I had to sit her down and explain her daddy hurt people...including her own mother.

"I know about that woman." Imogene narrowed her gaze.

I furrowed my brows. "What woman?"

"Claire Hale. Her death was all over the news a few weeks back. She's the same woman who came up to us when we were at the Peachtree Oyster House, isn't she?"

I parted my lips, unsure how to explain. I'd hoped Imogene was so busy with camp she wouldn't have had time to pay attention to the news.

I should have known better.

"Yes." I dropped my hold on her, sliding onto the barstool beside her. "That was Claire Hale."

I silently cursed my intelligent, observant daughter. The last thing I wanted was for Imogene to worry about the possibility that Nick was still hurting people. I was the parent here. It was my job to do the worrying for both of us.

Nick had already stolen so much of Imogene's childhood. I wouldn't allow him to steal her teenage years, too. It was impossible to shield her from everything life threw at her. But I could protect her from this. Could carry the burden for both of us. And that was precisely what I planned to do.

"She's also Lachlan Hale's sister," she continued. "He plays for—"

"I know who Lachlan Hale is."

Boy, did I ever.

"She committed suicide, Mama. Just like—"

I held up my hand. "It's not *him*, Imogene."

I refused to refer to Nick as her father. He lost that right the second he devalued another life.

"What I wanted to talk to you about has nothing to do with him. I promise."

She tilted her head. "But there *is* something you want to tell me?"

At the slight nervousness in her voice, I squeezed her leg. "It's a good thing. It just might take some...adjustment. It's a bit of a change for me."

"We're not moving, are we?"

"No. Nothing like that."

"Then what is it?"

I reached for her hand, gently grabbing it. "You know I love you very much, right? That you will always be my priority, no matter what?"

"I know...," she drew out, studying me warily.

"No matter what happens, that will never change. Every decision I make is with you in mind."

"Why are you telling me this? What's going on? Are you okay? Did something happen in Hawaii?"

I couldn't help but smile at the irony in her question. "Actually, baby, something *did* happen in Hawaii. Something good. Something exceptional, really."

"What is it? Is it the bakery? Was the opening a huge success?"

"Well, yes, it was. We're exploring the possibility of opening more locations on a few of the other islands. But that's not what I want to tell you."

I licked my lips, steeling myself for this conversation.

"You see, when I was in Hawaii, I kind of...met someone."

Her eyes widened, evidencing her initial shock. Then her expression turned more conniving. "Like, a guy?"

"Yes, Imogene," I replied, ignoring the teasing quality of her voice. "Most definitely a guy. Someone I've grown quite fond of, to be honest."

She stared at me for several moments, obviously surprised at my confession, especially now that she knew I wasn't joking. That this was real. That after years, I'd finally met someone.

Then she jumped off her stool and flung her arms

around me. "That's amazing, Mama!" she squealed. "I'm so happy for you."

She pulled back, eyes lit up with an enthusiasm I hadn't quite expected.

"Who is he? Is he from Hawaii? Is this a long-distance thing? Or was he there on vacation and lives somewhere on the mainland? What's he like? What's his name? How did you meet? Oh, my god. I want to know everything."

Before I could even attempt to answer, she hugged me again, bouncing on her toes, unable to contain her excitement.

"I'm just so stinking happy for you, Mama. You deserve this. So much."

I sighed, placing my hand on Imogene's back as I savored in her warmth and affection. "I love you, Imogene."

She allowed me to hold her for another moment, then pulled away, hoisting herself back onto her stool. Grabbing a piece of stromboli, she dipped it into the marinara sauce, then shoved it into her mouth, chewing a few moments before swallowing.

"Now, tell me everything about him. And don't leave out a single detail."

CHAPTER SEVEN

Julia

"I owe it all to a jellyfish," I tell Imogene, a dreamy smile crawling across my lips.

She scrunched her nose. "A...jellyfish?"

Reaching for the bottle of wine I'd opened, I poured a bit into a glass and took a sip.

"It's how we met. My first morning on Oahu, I stepped on one. He dug out the stingers."

"Ouch. Are you okay?" she asked, eyes darting to my leg.

"It was nearly three weeks ago. I'm as good as new. Don't get me wrong." I took another sip of wine. "It hurt like a bitch."

With a smirk, Imogene dropped her food onto her plate, holding out her hand. "That'll be a dollar."

I huffed out a breath, feigning annoyance. Regardless, I stood and reached into the back pocket of my shorts, withdrawing a bill from the stash I kept on me solely for this purpose.

I could act annoyed all I wanted, but the cash I gave her went toward a good cause.

A girl after my own heart, every year around Christmas, Imogene took all the money she'd earned, thanks to my colorful language, and we went toy shopping, which she would then donate to women's shelters in the area.

Most teenagers would probably want to buy something for themselves, such as designer clothes or the latest iPhone.

Not my girl.

It served as another reminder of what an amazing human she'd grown into.

"So... You stepped on a jellyfish. He came to your rescue. What happened next?"

"I went on my way. He went on his. But we kept running into each other."

"Aww..." She covered her heart with her hand, visibly swooning. "It's like fate wanted you to be together. It's so romantic."

At first, I certainly didn't think that was the case. Romance wasn't part of my initial arrangement with

Lachlan. But even that first night, when we were just two strangers who didn't know each other's real names, he'd romanced me.

Romance wasn't about grand declarations of love or passion-filled exchanges. It was in the little things.

Like the way he looked at me as if I were the only woman on earth, even in a crowd.

Or the way his hand always found mine, like he couldn't stand so much as a second passing without feeling my skin against his.

Or the way he put my comfort above all else, going so far as to bake a cake with me to help ease my nerves over the prospect of having sex for the first time in years.

"Wow...," Imogene exhaled, cutting through my thoughts.

"What?"

"I don't think I've seen you smile like this in, well...ever."

"I smile," I argued. "There are magazines all around the country filled with my smiling face."

"But that's Julia Prescott, the Baking Sweetheart of the South," she mimicked in a pronounced Southern drawl. Then she leveled her stare at me. "That's not really you. But right now..." She gestured at me. "This *is* you. It's a good look on you, Mama."

Her words left me momentarily speechless. Not just

at their content, but at the maturity Imogene possessed in order to come to that conclusion.

"Thanks, sweetie." I smiled before clearing my throat. "There's something else I should probably mention."

"What else is there? He makes you happy and treats you well, right?"

"He does."

"Then why do you look like you're about to tell me you're dating my teacher?" A look of horror crossed her expression. "Oh, my god. *Please* tell me it's not Mr. Marks. He's always flirting with you, and I know all the other girls think he's 'the hot teacher'. But I'd rather you not date any of my teachers. That would be really frigging weird."

"It's not Mr. Marks. Or any of your other teachers." I paused. "But it *is* someone you know. Or at least know of."

This caught her attention. "Who?"

I took a large sip of wine, then squared my shoulders, bracing myself for an epic meltdown of teenage proportions, as I'd named some of the shouting matches we'd gotten into, typically when I told her she couldn't go to a party at a friend of a friend's house I didn't know.

"Lachlan Hale."

She blinked, not moving, her expression unreadable, a talent she'd picked up from me. "Come again?"

I licked my lips, drawing in a deep breath. "His name is Lachlan Hale."

"That's what I thought you said," she replied, her voice distant as she stared into space for what felt like an eternity. Then she faced me again. "So, let me get this straight." She placed her hands on the island. "You stepped on a jellyfish, and a man named Lachlan Hale came to your rescue..."

"Yes."

"Would this happen to be the same Lachlan Hale who's a professional baseball player?"

"Yes."

"The same Lachlan Hale who's, like, fifteen years younger than you?"

"Thirteen," I corrected, "but yes."

She nodded, looking forward again, her demeanor still unreadable.

"I understand it's a lot, sweetie. Not only am I dating again after it's been only us for years, but I'm seeing someone who's, well, famous. Not to mention younger." My words started coming out faster as I attempted to win my daughter's support. "But he doesn't act younger. He's incredibly mature. And I actually had no idea who he was at first. I—"

"You're dating Lachlan *fucking* Hale?!" she shrieked.

I snapped my mouth shut, worried I'd see horror or

disgust on her face. But when she looked my way, all I saw was pure exhilaration.

"Imogene… Language," I attempted to berate her, but considering she'd heard me drop at least a dozen f-bombs before nine every morning, I doubted it had the desired effect.

"I appreciate your concern regarding my language, Mama, but if there's ever an occasion when swearing is entirely appropriate, it's when your mother tells you she's dating Lachlan *fucking* Hale! Oh, my god!"

"Is that a good 'Oh, my god'?"

"It's an *amazing* 'Oh, my god'." She flew off her barstool and flung her arms around me, squeezing tightly. Then she pulled back, eyes wide. "But his sister! Does he know she came up to you the day she died?"

Of course my observant daughter would put those pieces together. I just prayed she didn't put any more pieces together.

"Yes. He's aware."

"And he knows who you are?" She narrowed her gaze on me. "Your past?"

"He does. He knows all about…*him*. And trust me when I say the fact we ran into each other after his sister attempted to talk to me is just a coincidence. A remark-able coincidence, but a coincidence all the same. That's why he was in Hawaii the same time I was. He—"

"I know. He was on bereavement leave."

She studied me for a beat, taking a moment to process what I could only imagine to be a shock. "So you're really seeing Lachlan Hale?"

I nodded. "I'm really seeing Lachlan Hale."

She shook her head, mouth agape. Then she wrapped me in another hug, squeezing tightly.

"Does this mean you're not upset or weirded out about it?" I asked, holding her to me.

Pulling back, she met my eyes. "Why would I be upset?"

"I don't want this to affect you in any way, Imogene."

"How could it possibly affect me? Other than being able to go to as many games as we want." Her eyes widened. "Can he get us onto the field to hit some balls? That would be incredible. A dream come true. Hitting some balls under the lights of a professional field? I may die." Her words came out rapidly as she struggled to reel in her excitement, another trait she'd picked up from me. "Can Roman come, too? He's a huge fan. Like, massive. He's starting pitcher for the school team. Oh, my god. This may be the coolest thing you've ever done. Seriously."

I laughed. "I'm glad I'm now officially in the 'cool mom club'."

"Absolutely." She returned to her barstool, piling more food onto her plate. "I can't wait to tell everyone about this. It's so—"

"Imogene, sweetie..." I placed my hand over hers, stopping her. "I don't think that's such a good idea."

She furrowed her brows. "Why? You're his girl-friend, right?"

I parted my lips, her question throwing me off a bit. "Well... We've never exactly discussed titles. But yes, I suppose I am his girlfriend."

"Then what's the big deal?"

"The big deal is that *he's* a big deal."

"So? I don't..." She trailed off, her expression dropping. "It's because of *him*, isn't it?"

"Not entirely."

Nick certainly had a lot to do with my reasons for keeping my relationship with Lachlan quiet for now. Especially considering recent events. But he wasn't the *only* reason.

"Lachlan Hale isn't a regular person like you or me," I explained.

"You're not a regular person, either, Mama. People recognize you. You were a celebrity judge on a few of those baking competition shows."

"That's nothing compared to the massive following Lachlan has. His picture is plastered all over the city. People wear jerseys with his name and number on them. Hell, I'm pretty sure you have his fucking bobblehead in your room."

Before she could hold out her hand, I reached into

my pocket and pulled out the wad of cash, handing it over, hoping that would cover me for the rest of the night. I had a feeling there would be quite a bit of swearing on my part.

"Because of that, I need this to stay quiet. At least for now. It's for your own safety. The last thing I want is for word about our relationship to leak before we've made adequate preparations and for you to get pulled into this."

"So you're keeping it secret? From everyone?"

"A few people know. Like Naomi and your uncle. Now you. People I can trust not to share this. So I'm trusting *you* not to mention this to anyone. Not yet. This is new to both of us. We'd like some time for it to just be us. To give us a chance to get adjusted to a relationship with each other, as well as what it means for you. Then, when we're ready, we'll allow the world in. But not until."

She swept her analytical gaze over me, studying me for a few moments before nodding. "I can appreciate that." She grabbed my hand, squeezing it. "I'm really happy for you, Mama. I hope this is the start of something incredible for you."

"I hope so, too."

CHAPTER EIGHT

Lachlan

Exhaustion consumed me as I walked into my hotel room mere blocks from the White House, the Washington Monument visible from the immense windows.

After pitching eight innings, I was absolutely knackered. I typically didn't pitch more than six or seven, since the coaching staff kept a close eye on pitch count, not allowing any of us to go over one hundred.

But I had an amazing night. It took eight innings for me to reach one hundred. If Washington's renowned slugger hadn't gotten a base hit in the bottom of the fourth, I could have had another no-hitter under my belt, provided they kept me in and I continued pitching like I was.

But they didn't.

And now that the thrill of the game was over, I was beat.

After kicking off my shoes with a groan, I padded across the lush carpeting, slowly stripping off my suit jacket and tie. In a matter of moments, I was comfortably lounging on the bed in a pair of gym shorts, setting up the muscle-recovery device I used after each game, attaching a couple of electrodes to my left shoulder and arm.

Once I powered it up, I relaxed against the headboard and exhaled in relief as the machine massaged my muscles.

Glancing at the other side of the bed, I released a sigh, wishing Julia were here. Tonight was the first night in over a week I had to fall asleep without her. Hell, in the past three weeks, I was lucky enough to only have to spend two nights without her.

As much as I hated being away from her, we knew we had to eventually return to reality. This was it. Our new normal. I had to travel with the team. She had to be with her daughter. It didn't mean I couldn't miss her, though.

And I absolutely missed her. More than I thought possible.

Grabbing my phone off the nightstand, I debated sending her a text, even though it was after midnight and she was probably asleep. I wanted to let her know I was thinking about her.

That I missed her.

I navigated to my messages, about to type one out to Julia, when an incoming call flashed on my screen, Nikko's name popping up.

Since I'd returned to Atlanta, we'd exchanged the occasional text, but he hadn't called. Something told me his reason for calling after midnight my time had to be important.

"Cousin," I answered.

"*Howzit?* I caught bits and pieces of your game tonight. Congrats on another win."

"Thanks, man. I felt good. Could have stayed in to finish the game."

"That's what the closers are for," he reminded me, just as all my coaches often had to.

"I know. I know," I replied with a slight chuckle. Then there was a pause. "Is everything okay, Nikko? I doubt you just called to congratulate me on another win."

He expelled a long breath. "There's something I've been meaning to talk to you about but didn't want it to distract you from everything. But since you're away, presumably without any *distractions*, I figured this was probably the best time."

I sat up, turning off the recovery device so I could focus all my attention on him. "What is it?"

"I'm going to talk to my lieutenant and disclose everything we've learned. I was waiting to see if Agent Curran had uncovered anything new to help boost my argument about reopening the investigation into Piper's assault. From the sounds of it, he's hit a few dead ends, at least in his ability to convince local law enforcement to reopen their investigations. Maybe if we reopen ours, it might encourage others to do the same. Granted, Piper's death was a bit different from the other cases, which was why I wanted to speak with you first. Once the ball starts rolling, there's no stopping it. This *will* make headlines."

"I understand all of that. I just want the truth. Whoever broke into my home, attacked me, stabbed Claire, and brutally assaulted Piper is still out there. If Ethan's theory is correct, this bastard's harmed more women. Took more lives. I don't care about my name being connected to this. I want justice. For Claire. For Piper. And for Julia."

"Duly noted. Speaking of Julia..." His tone lightened. "How are things going?"

The anxiety that filled me mere seconds ago instantly vanished.

"Good." I smiled. "Really good. It's still kind of new, but we're figuring it out. Taking it one day at a time."

"That's all you can do in any relationship."

"Says the guy who hasn't been in one in years."

"What can I say? I'm married to my job. But in all seriousness... I'm happy for you, Lachlan. You deserve this. I'm just glad you finally realized that."

"And I'm just glad you finally smacked some sense into me."

"That's what I'm here for, bruh. Always happy to keep you on the straight and narrow.

"Anyway, I'm sure you're exhausted. I'll keep you posted about the investigation. If my lieutenant agrees to reopen, a detective will probably need to speak to you at some point. Verify your statement. Things like that."

"Thanks for the heads-up."

"You got it."

After ending the call, I dropped my phone onto the bed beside me, lying back and relaxing into the mattress. I closed my eyes, pushing down the unease over the idea of being forced to revisit every detail of that night.

But if it helped figure out who was behind all of this, I would do it.

Removing the electrodes from my shoulder and arm, I stowed the unit under the nightstand, about to turn off the light and get some rest. But I hated the idea of going to sleep without saying good night to Julia, so I fired off a quick text.

Me: *Good night, beautiful. Dream of me.*

I set my phone on the nightstand and turned off the light, wishing Julia were in my arms. Seconds later, my cell buzzed with an incoming text. I grabbed it, unlocking my screen.

Julia: *I always do.*

I couldn't fight the stupid grin that pulled on my lips.

Me: *Why are you still awake?*

Julia: *This ridiculously handsome baseball player I know was pitching tonight. I like staring at his ass in his uniform. It's better than watching porn.*

I barked out a laugh, warmth filling me.

Me: *I hope it was as good for you as it was for me.*

Julia: *It always is.*

I began to type out a response to ask how everything

went with her daughter today, but I missed hearing her voice. And I especially missed seeing her face.

So I flipped my light back on, then navigated to her contact and hit the FaceTime button. It took a few seconds, but Julia eventually appeared on my screen.

"You're a sight for sore eyes, gorgeous," I sighed. Her face was free from makeup, hair piled in a messy bun on top of her head. But I'd never seen anything so beautiful.

"It hasn't even been a day."

"Are you saying you haven't missed me even a little?"

"I didn't say that. I certainly *do* miss you. Especially now that I'm all alone in my bed."

I groaned, the image stirring my erection. An inconvenience, considering I'd have to take care of it myself.

"How did it go with your daughter today?" I hoped a change of subject would help.

"Better than expected, actually."

"What *did* you expect?"

"That she'd think I was crazy for dating someone so much younger, and a famous baseball player at that. Instead, she was incredibly supportive. Said I deserved to be happy."

"And you do. Like I said that first night together—"

"I know. I know." She playfully rolled her eyes. "To stop thinking about the age difference. That it didn't matter."

"Exactly. I don't care that you're older than me. When I look at you, I don't see your age. All I *do* see is an amazing woman I'm so damn attracted to it hurts."

A shy smile tugged on her lips.

"And when you look at me, I don't want you to only see some twenty-seven-year-old professional baseball player."

She flirtatiously batted her lashes. "What should I see?"

"That's up to you," I replied with a devious grin before my expression sobered. "But hopefully you see someone who cares about you, more than he thought he'd ever care about another person again." I held her gaze for a beat, then added, "And someone who gives you incredible orgasms."

She giggled, her smile reaching her eyes. "You most certainly do that." She pushed out a sigh. "How am I going to go four days without a single one?"

"Who said you had to?"

"I told you. I can't take off this weekend. Not with Imogene just getting home from camp. I promised to take her school shopping, since she starts back up in a few weeks. I—"

"No. I know that. That's not what I'm talking about."

Her brows furrowed. "Then what *are* you talking about?"

"Maybe it's time to be...self-indulgent." I adjusted myself on the bed, my arousal straining against my shorts at the mere thought. "I may not be there to get you off myself, but I can help you get *yourself* off."

She stared at me for what felt like an eternity. I wasn't sure how she'd respond to this proposition. Several weeks ago, she probably would have immediately shot it down, too nervous to do anything like this. But during our time together, she'd definitely become a lot more adventurous in the bedroom.

And in the shower.

And on the kitchen island.

And pretty much any surface we could enjoy each other on.

"Are you talking about..." She lowered her voice to a whisper, "phone sex?"

A low chuckle rumbled from my throat. "I am. Although I suppose a more appropriate term would be FaceTime sex. But yes, Julia. I want to help you get off." I bit my lower lip, my hand going to my erection. "Want to watch your face as you come. Want to jerk off knowing you're thinking about me when you touch that delicious pussy I plan on devouring the second I get home."

"Oh god." She closed her eyes as her head fell against the pillow. I could practically taste the desire radiating off her from hundreds of miles away.

"Come on, love. Let me make you feel good."

She kept her eyes shut for several long moments, my plea hanging in the silence.

Then she refocused her gaze on me, want and need swirling in her green orbs.

"Okay."

CHAPTER NINE

Julia

I couldn't believe I was going to do this. I'd never done anything remotely close to this before. Hell, before I met Lachlan, I'd rarely taken any time to be self-indulgent.

But if I'd learned anything during our short time together, Lachlan would never judge me. He'd never use anything I did or said against me. With him, I was free to be who I was always meant to be.

And, my god, the idea of doing something like this sent a thrill through me.

"Take off your shirt," Lachlan ordered, his voice husky with desire.

"Okay."

I set the phone on the bed and did as he instructed, tossing my t-shirt onto the floor. I grabbed my cell again and settled back against the pillows, my heart hammering at the sensation of my sheets against my bare flesh.

"Let me see you, gorgeous."

My breathing grew ragged and uneven, everything about this so damn erotic. I doubted it would take much to get me off tonight.

I slowly shifted my cell, allowing him to see my naked torso.

"Damn, baby."

When he groaned and bit his lower lip, I knew he was stroking his cock. It was the same expression that always came over his face whenever he readied himself to enter me. What I wouldn't give for him to be here. To thrust into me. To push my body to its limits.

Hell, past its limits.

"Touch your breast."

"Not my clit?"

"No, baby. Not yet. I'm going to fucking torture you, because being so far from you is such a cruel torture for me. Cruel and beautiful and agonizing at the same time."

"My god," I whimpered, hand cupping my breast, instinct and craving taking over as I kneaded the flesh.

"Fuck, that's hot." His voice grew excited, more breathy. "Pinch your nipple. Pretend it's my teeth."

I took my nipple between my thumb and forefinger, giving it a gentle tug.

"Harder."

I licked my lips, squeezing a little more.

"Harder," he grunted, jaw clenched, muscles tense.

"Go easy or you're going to come," I teased.

"I'm not even bloody touching myself yet."

"You're not?"

"Trust me. It's an exercise in extreme restraint. As much as I love being first at my job, I always plan on coming second with you. Now, squeeze that nipple harder."

I did as he asked, throwing my head back as I reveled in the sensation, squeezing my thighs together in search of some sort of release.

Release I feared Lachlan was in no hurry to give me.

"Remember our first night together?" he asked. "How hard you came when I finger fucked you and bit your nipple at the same time."

"How could I forget?" I panted, tugging my nipple harder, wishing it were enough to extinguish the flames coursing through me. But I doubted anything could.

"God, you were so fucking beautiful once you finally let loose with me. That's what I want with you, Julia. Want you to let loose. Forget all the rules and be free."

"I want that, too," I exhaled, writhing, desperately chasing my release. "What I need. Now, let me be free."

"Take off your shorts," he demanded.

I didn't even hesitate, tossing my cell beside me and quickly shoving my shorts down my legs.

"That was quick," Lachlan mused once I brought the phone up again.

"You've got me all worked up. Time to make good on your promise to help me get off."

"I plan on it. Place your feet on the mattress and spread your legs."

I followed his instructions, electricity coursing through me when I imagined him burying his face between my thighs, much like he did right before he left town.

"Now what?"

"Do you want to touch yourself?"

"You know I do."

"Say it."

"I want to touch myself."

"Where?" he shot back with a smirk. "Your head? Your arm? Your toe? What part of your body are you desperate to touch?"

"My pussy. God..." I bucked my hips, needing to feel something. Anything.

It boggled my mind to think I'd gone years without sex, sometimes weeks without even considering taking care of my own needs.

But after being with Lachlan that first time, I could barely go twelve hours without needing to get off. He may have initially called me Belle, but he most certainly unleashed the beast hidden deep within me.

"Let me touch myself, Lachlan. I can't... I can't take it anymore. I need to get off. Need you to get off with me."

"I'll never deprive you of your needs." He tilted the screen, giving me a glimpse of his throbbing erection as he stroked it.

"My god," I moaned, trailing my hand down my torso and between my thighs, spreading my slickness around. "I miss that cock. Miss feeling it inside me. The way you move..."

I slipped a finger inside me, trying to replicate the sensation of fullness I experienced whenever Lachlan was inside me. But a finger was woefully inadequate to compete with his impressive size.

"You drive me wild. Make me feel things I didn't think possible."

"Goddamn, baby," Lachlan hissed, the muscles in his face tensing as his breathing increased even more. "Tell me more. Tell me what you're doing."

"Touching my pussy."

"More. I need details."

"I'm rubbing my clit."

"Taste yourself," he grunted.

I brought my finger to my lips, making an elaborate show out of licking my essence off it.

"Julia..." His expression became strained. Almost pained. "I need you to touch yourself again. Imagine I'm fucking you from behind as you rub your clit."

"Oh god," I exhaled, the picture he painted pushing me higher and higher.

"Do you know how good you feel that way? Every time I slam into you from behind, feel your pussy walls constrict around me..." He licked his lips, facial muscles tensing as he fought against his own orgasm. "It's heaven, love. Fucking heaven. That's what being with you feels like. Like I'm in fucking heaven. Nothing's ever felt so good. So right. You were made for me. I feel it in my heart. Now, give me your orgasm. Come for me, beautiful."

His words set me off, my body as much a slave to him from hundreds of miles away as it was when he was inside me. Eyes squeezed shut, I bit my lower lip to muffle my cries as I shook and quivered through my orgasm.

"That's right, baby. I'm the only one who can make you feel this way. Never forget it."

"Never," I assured him, amazed at just how intense an orgasm he was able to pull out of me without laying a single finger on me.

This wasn't the first time I'd touched myself. I wasn't a prude. But, god... I didn't know phone sex could be so fucking incredible.

"Let me watch you," I said, body still tingling. "I want to watch you come."

Within seconds, he released an anguished cry, his phone shaking as he jerked through his own release, my name on his tongue a cross between a benediction and a curse.

Neither one of us said anything for several moments as we attempted to get our breathing under control.

"How was it?" he finally asked. "You're not freaked out, are you?"

"Actually, no." I smiled. "I quite enjoyed myself."

"As did I. Hell, I *more* than enjoyed myself. Even from a couple hundred miles away, you drive me wild, Julia."

He ran a hand over his face, shaking his head, staring at me in awe. "What are you doing to me? I barely recognize the person I was just a few weeks ago."

"I feel the same about myself."

He sighed, rolling over onto his side, as he typically did after making love to me. I did, as well, facing the side of the bed he slept on, propping my phone up on the pillow, as if he were here with me.

"Are you happy with me?" he asked. I could almost feel his hand skimming down my frame.

"Deliriously so."

"Good. You make me..." He sighed. "I'm not sure there's a word in the English language to properly describe how I feel when I'm with you."

"How about in Hawaiian?"

He furrowed his brows. "Hawaiian?"

"Yeah."

He contemplated for a beat, then smiled. "Actually, there was this saying my mum often said. A well-known Hawaiian phrase."

"What's that?"

"'*He 'olina leo ka ke aloha.*'"

"I understood the *aloha*, but that's it. What does it mean?" I rested my head in my hand, sighing contentedly.

"'Joy is in the voice of love.' I never really understood it."

He focused his intense gaze on mine, so many emotions swirling within. Including one I didn't think possible so soon.

"Until now."

CHAPTER TEN

Julia

"Ms. Prescott," a voice clipped out the second Wes and I stepped into the coffee shop around the block from Wes' office in Downtown Atlanta on Sunday morning.

When I spied Agent Curran sitting at a table in the corner, Ethan beside him, unease filled me. I knew Ethan had offered to assist Agent Curran in his investigation, allowed him access to everything he and Claire had uncovered in the hopes it would help him figure out what happened to not only her, but over a dozen other women.

Still, I couldn't shake the feeling there was another

reason for Ethan's presence. And why we were meeting here.

In the seven years I'd known the federal agent, he'd never asked to meet anywhere but his office.

Wes touched a hand to my elbow, giving me a reassuring smile as he steered me across the busy coffee shop.

"Mr. Bradford." Agent Curran stood and offered Wes his hand. "Good to see you again. I just wish it were under different circumstances."

"As do I," Wes answered, then shifted his attention to the lanky blond at his side. "You must be Ethan."

"Ethan Shore." He held out his hand for Wes, the two shaking cordially. "Nice to meet you. Julia speaks very highly of you."

"Thank you."

"Have a seat." Agent Curran gestured to the two chairs opposite him and Ethan. It didn't escape my notice there were no files on the table. No notepads. Nothing.

Which increased my gut feeling that this wasn't exactly a meeting to discuss the progress he'd made on the case. If anything, I feared he was about to tell me there wasn't a case. But Ethan's presence made me question that, too. I'd witnessed his tenacity firsthand. He wasn't going to walk away from this without a fight.

"Thank you for coming down here today, and on a weekend." Agent Curran adjusted his tie.

It may have been a Sunday, but the dark suit, light blue button-down, and black tie made it appear as if this were any other workday for him. Come to think of it, I couldn't recall ever seeing him wearing anything other than a dark suit and blue shirt.

"It's not a problem at all," I said with a forced smile. "Especially if you've been able to get some answers."

He licked his lips, his expression falling.

"*Were* you able to get answers?" I glanced at Wes, noting his own unease. "Wes mentioned you were able to confirm that two other pieces of jewelry I'd received did, in fact, belong to two of the other victims on Claire's list."

"That's true," Agent Curran replied evenly. "Unfortunately, I'm being asked to...walk away. At least temporarily."

"Walk away?" Wes repeated. "Why? This is a serious matter." He lowered his voice, leaning across the table. "There's a potential serial killer out there repeating Nick's kill cycle. But you're telling me the FBI is just going to walk away? Isn't this what you do? Chase serial killers and bring them to justice?"

"As a matter of point, serial killers aren't as pervasive as they once were. Not with all the forensic advances we've made over the past several decades. But that's not the issue here."

"Then what *is* the issue?" Wes pressed. "Why are you abandoning this when you know there's something here?"

"Trust me. I don't like it any more than you do. But there are jurisdictional concerns." Agent Curran looked from Wes to me. "As much as I wish I could order every local law enforcement agency to reopen their investigation, I can't. Homicide investigations are strictly the province of local and state law enforcement. The only time the FBI can get involved is if there's evidence of serial murder—"

"Which there is," Wes insisted.

"*And* we're invited in by the local powers that be." He leveled his stare on my brother. "That hasn't happened here. Not yet. While I did reach out to each individual jurisdiction, most of them weren't happy with the idea of some outside agency coming in and telling them their initial determination of suicide was wrong, especially when my assertion is based on what some would consider a pretty tenuous theory that most likely wouldn't even satisfy a single judge enough to issue an arrest warrant."

"*Tenuous?*" Wes shot back. "What about the fact that each time, an important piece of jewelry came up missing after they allegedly took their life? On the same day as one of Nick's victims did the same? And that piece of jewelry ended up being sent to Julia? How could that be considered 'tenuous'?"

"It's certainly something," Agent Curran assured us. "But local law enforcement agencies want more than a connection that could be described as circumstantial, at best. Their case files are filled with indisputable scientific evidence supporting their determination that these women took their own lives. I need more than a piece of jewelry, which anyone could have replicated after even a cursory look through their social media profiles. Not to mention, these women were from different backgrounds. Different races. Different ages. Hell, a few of them even identified with different sexual orientations."

"But they each shared a characteristic with one of Nick's victims," Wes argued. "And allegedly took their life on the same date as in Nick's case. That's got to count for something."

"And it does. But in conducting my due diligence, I ran some numbers, just to see what we're dealing with here."

He pulled a pair of glasses and a small notebook out of the inside pocket of his jacket. After sliding on the glasses, he flipped open the notebook, stopping when he found what he was searching for.

"Suicide is the tenth leading cause of death in this country. On average, approximately 150 people die by suicide every day." He looked up. "Every. Day," he repeated to emphasize his point. "So let's look at this, starting with March third."

There was a slight tremble in his voice as he uttered the date, considering it was the day his niece, Annabelle, took her life all those years ago.

"Do you know how many people in this country committed suicide on March third of this year?" He looked at us, pausing for a beat. "187. And of those 187, seventy-five were female. And of those seventy-five, half were college students."

He closed the notebook, returning it, along with his glasses, to his pocket. Then he leaned across the table, his gray eyes intense.

"Do you see what I'm getting at here? While it's suspicious, it's not enough. Not for local law enforcement agencies to consider the possibility they were wrong. That their forensics were wrong. We need more to go on. Until then..." He shook his head, "I'm afraid there's nothing I can do."

"So it's over?" I asked, trying to mask my frustration.

While I wasn't sure what I'd hoped Agent Curran would share with me, I hadn't expected to learn there would be absolutely *no* investigation. I understood Claire's theory wasn't iron-clad, that there could be another explanation for everything. But my gut said there was something to it.

"What about Nikko? Detective Kekoa?" I corrected. "He's Piper Kekoa's older brother and a homicide detective. Confirmed the jewelry I received five years ago belonged to his sister. Can't you reach out to him? See if he can invite you in or something?"

"I spoke with Detective Kekoa yesterday," Agent Curran responded.

His even tone was at complete odds with the dread settling in my stomach over the prospect of this continuing for months, maybe years. Of getting a phone call telling me I'd received another package. Another piece of jewelry taken from another woman who was no longer breathing.

"What did he say?" Wes inquired.

"His department is currently evaluating whether to reopen the investigation into the home invasion that resulted in Ms. Kekoa's death. His lieutenant hasn't made her final decision, but considering Ms. Kekoa's ties to law enforcement, my guess is it's likely they will."

"So that's good," I said. "They can invite you to help then, right?"

"Perhaps they eventually will. But they'll want to conduct their own investigation first. Hopefully it will uncover something that could tie Ms. Kekoa's death to these other women."

"Other than the fact Julia was sent her necklace," Wes snapped.

"Yes," Agent Curran calmly answered. "But as I've reminded you, there's no physical evidence connecting the women to those pieces of jewelry. I'm not trying to burst your bubble, but it's important to play devil's advocate so we know what we're up against. It's possible for someone to argue that an individual saw a story about a woman committing suicide, fixated on that woman, saw a social media photo of her wearing a particular piece of jewelry, and decided to have a replica made to send to Julia."

Wes opened his mouth, most likely to argue the ridiculousness of that theory, but Agent Curran held up his hand, stopping him before he could get a word out.

"I understand it's a stretch, especially considering family members did indicate a certain piece of jewelry was missing after their death. I'm simply trying to give you the arguments we can expect. That I've already faced."

"So we're just supposed to sit around and do nothing while this guy targets another woman to kill on October thirteenth?" I shook my head, the entire scenario feeling patently unfair.

"I didn't say that," Agent Curran stated, lips twitching with the hint of a smile. "I simply said *my* hands were tied in this matter at present. Luckily, we know someone with investigative skills who doesn't have the same restrictions I do." He glanced toward Ethan.

"You're going to help?" I asked him.

Ethan nodded. "Of course. I want justice for Claire. I won't stop until I get it."

"Mr. Shore doesn't have to answer to anyone but himself," Agent Curran explained. "So he's offered to continue the investigation Claire began. Comb through every aspect of these women's lives. Something connects them. We're going to turn over every single leaf until we figure out what that is.

"Once we do, we'll find this bastard and make him pay."

CHAPTER ELEVEN

Lachlan

As I slid into the back seat of my chauffeured car after landing in Atlanta late Monday night, I wasted no time before ringing Julia. I should have just let her sleep, considering she had to get up early for work tomorrow.

But I ached to see her again. Hated the idea of being mere miles away and not being able to touch her.

"Hey." Her husky voice came over the line.

"Hey, gorgeous."

"Are you back in town?"

"I am. I don't think I've ever been so happy to be home."

"I'm glad you're home, too. I missed you."

"And I missed you. Can I come over?"

There was a brief silence. Then she expelled a long breath. "I don't know, Lachlan. I want nothing more than to see you, but it's not like before. I'm not sure Imogene's first introduction to the new man in her mother's life should be the morning after he spends the night."

"I just want to see you, Julia. I'll set an alarm. Leave before she wakes up. She'll be none the wiser. It'll be like we're in high school. Sneaking around behind our parents' backs. Having to be super quiet." I chuckled. "I'll even go out through the window to give you the full experience."

"And risk you breaking your pitching arm? I'm not sure I want that on my conscience."

"It's okay. My arm is insured for millions."

"Your...*arm* is insured?"

"Crazy, isn't it?"

"I've heard crazy things. Hell, I've *lived* crazy things. But learning your *arm* is insured... That's a whole new level of insane."

I snorted. "Tell me about it. So, what do you say? Can I come see you? I'm only home for three days before I have to go on the road again. I want you every chance I can get."

She was silent a moment before growling softly in resignation. "Fine. But you have to promise you'll be gone first thing in the morning. I'm serious about this, Lachlan."

"Is that your mom voice?" I teased. "It's incredibly sexy. Use it again. Are you going to put me in timeout?"

"Oh, my god. Stop it. You're so bad."

"And in thirty minutes, you'll find out exactly how bad I can be."

"I can't wait."

"Me, either. See you soon, love."

I lingered on the line for a beat. Once she ended the call, I returned my phone to my pocket.

The twenty-minute drive from the airport to my place seemed like the longest of my life.

Once my driver pulled into the driveway, I didn't even wait for him to open my door, jumping out of the car. After a cursory nod of thanks, I grabbed my things and hurried into the house, dropping my suitcase in the foyer before heading into the attached garage.

Keys in hand, I climbed into my Audi SUV, making the four-mile drive to Julia's house in Brookhaven in a matter of minutes. I was about to pull into her driveway, but hesitated, unsure if I should park there.

Opting to play it safe, I parked on the street, then jogged up to the front door. As I raised my hand to knock, I paused, unsure if I should do that, either. Thankfully, I didn't have to think about it for long, the door opening.

A sense of comfort instantly washed over me, the sight of Julia stealing my breath. She was dressed in a pair of shorts and a t-shirt with "Fueled by wine, tacos, and sarcasm" across the front. It was a little thing, but whenever I saw her in one of those t-shirts, it truly felt like I was finally home.

"Sorry." I ran a hand through my hair. "I wasn't sure if I should knock or—"

Before I could utter another word, she grabbed my tie, yanking me toward her. Her lips crashed against mine, our tongues tangling in a kiss that heated every inch of me, my need for her increasing with every second. I pulled her close, the warmth of her body against mine an aphrodisiac for my soul.

"Miss me?" I panted once she brought our kiss to an end.

"You have no idea. And then you show up in a suit? It makes me want to crawl on top of you right now."

"Well then..."

Crooking a wry smile, I walked her backward into the house, kicking the door closed behind me. When her back hit the wall, I pinned her to it, sensually circling my hips so she could feel how desperate I was for her.

"I'm all yours to do whatever your filthy little heart desires."

My lips collided with hers, lust coiling within me. I was hopelessly addicted to her taste. Her kiss. Her everything. When I dipped my fingers just below the waist-band of her shorts, her muscles clenched under my touch.

She tore her mouth from mine, breaths coming fast and heavy as she placed her hands on the lapels of my jacket.

"Bedroom. Now."

"Yes, ma'am." I stepped away from her, extending my arm toward the open living area. "Lead the way."

Since returning to Atlanta, we'd spent all our time at my house. I hadn't really questioned it. I liked having her there. It made my place feel more like a home.

But as she grabbed my hand and led me up the stairs, the walls covered with photographs of Imogene, I wondered if that had something to do with it. If she'd hoped to keep this part of herself from me for some reason.

I didn't want to think that was the case. After all, I had nothing to base it off of. This was new territory for both of us... In more ways than one.

Reaching the top of the stairs, I came to a stop in front of a framed collage of a slender blonde playing soccer. "Is this her?" I whispered, gesturing to it. "Your daughter?"

Julia followed my line of sight, even though it didn't matter *where* I looked. All the photos in this house appeared to be of her daughter. It was obvious how important she was to her.

"That's Imogene. Or Mo, as she often goes by these days."

I stepped toward the collage, studying her. There was no mistaking the resemblance. "She looks just like you. Apart from the eye color. And hair color."

"Well, mine's naturally blonde, too."

"I know," I said, recalling the image of a beaten Julia taken in the aftermath of Nick's attack. "But she has your smile," I continued, pushing down the anger bubbling to the surface over the reminder of everything she'd endured.

"Thank you." She flashed me a smile before her expression grew heated.

Sauntering up to me, she grasped my tie, fingers working to loosen it. "Now. Do you plan on standing out here all night? Or do you want to come to the bedroom?" She yanked the tie free. "Maybe put this to some...other use."

"Bedroom," I growled. "Definitely the fucking bedroom."

She placed a finger over my mouth, hushing me. Then she took my hand and pulled me into the room at the end of the hallway, softly closing the door behind her.

When she turned around to face me, we lunged at

each other like two horny teenagers who found themselves home alone.

We tore at each other's clothes, desperate to feel flesh against flesh after too long apart. It had only been four days, but that long with her was akin to torture.

Once I pushed my boxer briefs down my legs, eliminating the final article of clothing between us, Julia grabbed my erection, stroking me against her heat.

"I need you inside me. To hell with foreplay."

I hardened even more, my pulse skyrocketing. She barely resembled the unsure, shy woman she was less than a month ago. The one who blushed at the mere idea of talking about sex. I couldn't help but feel a hint of pride at how open she was now. How free she was around me.

It made me want more of this.

To give her wings.

To make her fly.

"Keep stroking me like that, and I won't last long enough for foreplay."

"Well then..."

Placing a hand against my chest, she pushed me across the room until the back of my legs hit the bed. I lowered myself onto it, about to lie down, but she stopped me.

"No. Like this." She crawled on top of me, a leg on either side as I remained in a sitting position.

She raised herself slightly, the warmth between her thighs igniting me. I moved my cock against her a few times, spreading her desire around. Then I met her eyes, nodding. She lowered herself onto me, both of us sighing in relief at that sensation of fullness we'd missed these past few days.

"So damn good, baby," I moaned as she pulsed against me. I ran my hand up her torso, kneading her breasts.

From the beginning, I thought Julia was one of the most beautiful women I'd ever seen. But right now, watching as she chased her pleasure, back arched, eyes closed, I'd never seen anything so damn sexy.

I had no idea what I did to be the lucky bastard to be able to give her this. To *experience* this with her.

But I wasn't going to question it. I was going to enjoy it for as long as I could.

Maybe even forever.

CHAPTER TWELVE

Julia

A chiming cut through the serenity of my bedroom, stirring me from sleep. I inhaled, stretching, my entire body aching.

But it was a good ache.

A great ache.

A fucking marvelous ache.

One that grew stronger the second Lachlan snaked his arm along my waist and pulled me against his body.

"Why does it feel like we just fell asleep?" His voice had a raspiness to it, evidencing his exhaustion. Thankfully, he wasn't scheduled to pitch again until tomorrow, giving him one more day to rest up.

Because last night, he most certainly did *not* rest.

"We *did* just fall asleep," I reminded him. "Someone couldn't keep his cock out of me."

He thrust gently against me, ready to go another round. "I had to make up for lost time."

"If this is what I have to look forward to when you come back from a few away games, you should go out of town more often."

"You think so?"

"Well, last night *was* pretty amazing. And..." I trailed off.

"What is it?" When I didn't answer, he buried his head in my neck, his unshaven jawline scraping against my skin. "Tell me."

"I also had fun with you when you were out of town."

"Hmm..." He kissed along my neck and shoulder, his fingers caressing my torso becoming more sensual by the second. "What about it was fun? Getting off with me on the phone?"

"Yes," I moaned from a combination of the memory and Lachlan's hand inching farther south, my core clenching in anticipation.

"If I touched you right now, would you be wet from thinking about it?"

I closed my eyes, breathing growing ragged. I should stop him, insist we couldn't do this. Not now. Not when he needed to leave before Imogene woke up.

But when his hand neared my sex, all rational thought disappeared, my decisions driven by one thing, and one thing only.

Desire.

"Why don't you find out?" I bent my knee, propping a leg up in invitation. I held my breath as his hand traveled the last inch, so close to touching me.

But then he pulled back, leaving me bereft and wild with need, which only increased when he took my earlobe between his teeth.

"Show me," he growled.

"Show you what?"

He pushed me onto my back and hovered over me. His eyes were lazy from lack of sleep, his dark hair disheveled. But in the early morning light filtering through the windows, he was absolutely beautiful, all sinewy muscle and strong features.

I still couldn't believe this man chose me out of all the women he could be with. I often found myself questioning it, but I was trying to break free from my past. That included a lifetime of thinking I was mediocre. That I wasn't good enough. Lachlan proved to me that I was.

His lips skimmed mine in a ghost of a kiss that made me hungry for more. "I only got to see your face when you touched yourself during our...chat. So I want to watch you touch yourself. Want to see all of you."

I blinked, heart racing at the notion. It was one thing to do that when all he saw was my face. When he was miles away.

It was another thing to do it when he was right in front of me, watching my every move.

"Please, love." He nuzzled my neck again, teeth nipping my skin. "For me." He pulled back and met my eyes. When I didn't immediately agree, he grabbed my hand. "Here. I'll help you get started." He arched a brow, waiting.

I could have said no. Taken the out he was giving me. But the way he looked at me with so much lust and need... I couldn't turn him down.

Heart thrashing in my chest, I gave him a subtle nod, the atmosphere in the room becoming even more heated. His powerful gaze trained on me, he trailed my hand along my torso, smoothing it over my chest.

"Squeeze them," he whispered, his breath hot against my neck.

I did as he asked, massaging my breast, then pinching my nipple.

"Fuck, Julia." He brought his body closer to mine, his erection throbbing against my thigh. "So damn hot." He peppered kisses along my neck and shoulder. "You are just so damn hot."

I moaned, the combination of his words and the feeling of my hand on me ratcheting up my desire higher than I thought possible, considering *he* wasn't even touching me. But knowing he was watching me do this ignited an inferno inside me.

"Touch your pussy. Let me see how wet you are for me."

I bit my bottom lip, slowly lowering my hand down my stomach before bringing it between my thighs, spreading my desire around.

"Push a finger inside."

I followed his demand, inserting a finger at the same time as I rubbed my thumb against my clit.

"Oh god," I whimpered.

I never thought I'd be the type of woman to do something like this. Hell, I didn't think I'd be the type of woman to have phone sex with her hot, younger boyfriend. But I couldn't stop even if he asked me to.

"That's it, baby," he grunted.

I didn't have to open my eyes to know he was stroking his erection. I heard it in his voice. Felt him as he rubbed it against my hip.

"Fuck yourself with your finger."

"Lachlan," I moaned. "It's so..."

"Hot. That's what it is. You are so fucking hot." He brought a hand to my chest, lowering his mouth to my nipple.

I didn't think I could possibly experience any more

pleasure than I had seconds ago at the knowledge of him watching me touch myself. I was wrong.

Lust and desire collided in a riotous combination as he took my nipple between his teeth, nibbling somewhat harshly.

I struggled to catch my breath, too many sensations filling me.

"You're close, aren't you?"

I nodded quickly, that familiar sensation growing stronger and stronger with each stroke, each nip.

I thrust against my fingers, on the precipice of coming undone, when he suddenly grasped my wrist, pulling my hand away.

Flinging my eyes open, I gaped at Lachlan in disbelief as he pinned my wrists on either side of my head.

And I thought it was a cruel form of punishment to go four days without feeling him inside me. But this was worse. So close, then deprived of what I desperately needed.

Gaze unwavering, he crawled between my legs. A whimper fell from my throat when he pressed his arousal against my clit, teasing and torturing.

"Ask me to make you come."

"Lachlan...," I moaned, flexing my hands as he kept my wrists locked in place.

He lowered his lips. I craned my head, chasing his kiss, his touch, his anything. But at the last second, he shifted, wrapping his mouth around my finger, licking off my desire.

"Absolutely delicious." He made a show of running his tongue along his lips, then turned his penetrating stare back to me. "Now. Ask me to make you come, Julia." He circled his hips, his erection hitting that bundle of nerves once more.

"Please, Lachlan. Will you make me come?"

He brought his mouth to mine, our tongues tangling in an erotic dance. Then he thrust inside me.

Forgetting where I was, I let out a scream, the relief at feeling him all-consuming.

Lachlan covered my mouth with his, swallowing my cries. "Shh... Quiet."

"Stop fucking me so good and I won't scream like that."

As he rotated his hips more sensually, hitting the spot that drove me wild, my eyes rolled into the back of my head.

"Never, Julia." His slow motions were achingly perfect as I neared that peak once more. "I will never stop making you feel good."

"Oh god...," I exhaled, meeting every push, every thrust.

"Let go, baby. Give me your pleasure."

Overcome with sensation, I wrapped my legs around

his waist, on the verge of shattering into a thousand pieces.

Then the door flung open.

"Mama, are you okay? I heard—"

"Fuck!" I shrieked at the same time as Lachlan rolled off me, yelling, "Shite!"

Heart racing, I grabbed the duvet, covering myself just as I looked up to see a wide-eyed Imogene standing in the doorway.

I opened my mouth, unsure what to say.

"Well... That explains the screaming." She spun around, running from the room, slamming the door behind her.

I stared at the ceiling, body throbbing from my stolen orgasm, as well as the embarrassment of my daughter walking in on us.

Then a low chuckle cut through the silence.

I glanced to my right, wanting to berate Lachlan, tell him it wasn't funny. But when he wrapped an arm around me and pulled me into his embrace, I couldn't help but join in. He wasn't to blame. It took two to tango. And I most certainly tangoed with him this morning.

"Why do I feel like my parents just caught me with a boy's tongue down my throat, but on a much more embarrassing level?" I mused.

"Because your daughter just walked in and saw my cock inside you."

"Not helping, Lachlan."

"I'm sorry." He placed a soft kiss on my head, the sweet gesture at complete odds with the way he just fucked me. "You wanted me to leave early for a reason."

"It's my fault. I forgot myself for a minute."

On a long sigh, I extracted myself from his arms and stood. Padding over to the dresser, I opened the drawers, pulling out a fresh shirt and pair of shorts.

"I need to go talk to her. Make sure she's okay. She's probably dousing her eyes with bleach. Not from seeing you," I rambled nervously as I yanked a t-shirt over my head, then the shorts up my legs. "But from walking in on her mother having sex. That'll scar any kid for life."

"Want me to come with you?"

I met his eyes and smiled. "I need to do this on my own. Don't want to make it any more awkward than it needs to be."

"Of course."

He let out an uneasy laugh as he ran a hand through his hair. "Nothing like being forced back to reality. Guess we had to come down from the clouds at some point, huh?"

"If it's a little too real for you, I understand." I averted my gaze, fidgeting with the hem of my t-shirt. "When you first agreed to my proposition, I highly doubt this was what you had in mind. Some single mom with a fourteen-year-old daughter. Because, let me tell you, she certainly has her moments that make you want to rip out your hair and scream. She's a teenager. And a girl. She is a master at the annoyed glare. Not to mention—"

A hand on my bicep caught me by surprise. I darted my eyes to see Lachlan standing next to me. He brushed his lips against mine, the simple gesture erasing my worries.

"I meant what I told you in Hawaii. And I'll say it today and every day going forward if that's what it takes to finally get it through this thick, beautiful skull of yours."

He placed his hand against my back and pulled my body close. Touching my chin, he lifted my eyes to his.

"I want to be with you, Julia. That includes everything and everyone important to you. Like Imogene."

He held my gaze for a moment, allowing his statement to sink in. Then his sinful mouth curved into a sly smile.

"We'll just have to learn to be a bit more quiet when I'm screwing you."

I burst out laughing, my anxiety and unease about this situation momentarily waning.

Then his expression sobered once again. "But in all seriousness... I understand this will be an adjustment. For all of us. It won't be perfect, and we'll make some mistakes. But we'll figure it out. Together. Okay?"

I placed my hand on his chest, relishing in the

comforting *thump-thump* of his heart. Could this man be any more perfect? I kept waiting to learn he had some horrible flaw. That he had a secret obsession with creepy clowns. That he slurped his soup.

So far, though, I'd yet to uncover anything.

With a sigh, I tilted my head back, lips skimming his. "Okay."

CHAPTER THIRTEEN

Julia

Approaching Imogene's door, I paused and took a deep breath, steeling myself for whatever conversation we were about to have.

She wasn't ignorant when it came to sex. I made sure of it. I was raised in a somewhat conservative house where sex wasn't discussed. When teenage hormones hit, I certainly made quite a few bad decisions. All because I didn't have any sort of parental figure to explain sex to me. That it was something to be celebrated, enjoyed.

So when I ended up married to a man who used sex to control me, manipulate me...punish me, I thought that was normal.

It wasn't until I met Lachlan that I realized how amazing sex could be.

Imogene was still young. While I hoped she wouldn't become sexually active anytime soon, I didn't want her to feel like she couldn't talk to me about it. Didn't want her to feel ashamed about having certain urges. Not like I was made to feel at her age.

Bringing my hand up, I knocked gently, expecting to hear rustling from within. When I didn't, I knocked again, then cracked open the door, peeking my head inside her room.

"Imogene, sweetie?"

Obviously sensing motion out of the corner of her eye, she darted her gaze to mine from where she sat cross-legged on her bed, laptop and phone in front of her.

She pulled her AirPods out of her ears and returned them to their case.

"Sorry." She smiled slightly. "I had my music turned up loud. Figured I'd give you privacy to, well...finish."

My face heated, but I pushed down my embarrassment, knowing we needed to have this conversation.

"I'm sorry you had to walk in on that." I padded across the room and sat on the corner of her bed. "That wasn't exactly how I planned on you meeting Lachlan for the first time."

"You and me both." She crossed her arms in front of her chest, looking down at her body.

Imogene was like every other teenage girl on the planet. Constantly uneasy in her own skin. Always comparing herself to everyone. Feeling inadequate in every way.

While she was taller than most girls her age, and even a majority of the boys, she was a bit late in developing. She'd be fifteen in a few months. But she hadn't exactly grown breasts yet. Not like many of her friends. It made her extremely self-conscious.

I tried to tell her she'd eventually have huge boobs like her mom and would wish they'd disappear, especially during that time of the month. That didn't stop her from comparing herself to other girls, though.

"Are you okay with what you saw? I mean, not *okay* okay. No one wants to walk in on their mom having sex. I'm sure you'd prefer to think you were conceived through some sort of immaculate conception. But I just wanted—"

"You're doing it again."

I shifted my eyes to hers. "Doing what?"

She laughed slightly, tugging at her t-shirt in an effort to hide her own body. Something else she probably picked up from me.

"Rambling when you're nervous. And it's okay. I

mean, I would have preferred to *not* walk in on you getting freaky first thing in the morning—"

"Getting freaky? How do you even—"

She placed her hand over mine. "But I think it's pretty awesome you're having sex. And, judging from the sounds, enjoying it quite a bit."

"Imogene!" I exclaimed, aghast.

I fully expected her to be embarrassed over the entire situation. Never in my wildest imagination would I have thought she'd essentially cheer me on.

"It's like you told me, Mama. Sex isn't anything to be ashamed of. It's a healthy aspect of your emotional well-being."

I stared at her for several moments, speechless at how level-headed she was about this. There were so many times I often felt like I was the child and she was the adult.

I scooted up to the head of the bed, pulling her into my arms. Thankfully, she decided to not act like an annoyed teenager, allowing me to snuggle her.

"How am I lucky enough to have such an awesome daughter?"

"Easy. I was raised by a kick-ass mom."

I opened my mouth to berate her for swearing, but given the events of the morning, I figured she was owed a few free passes. Instead, I just enjoyed the feeling of her in my arms, fully aware moments like these were fleeting.

"But seriously..." She pulled out of my embrace and met my eyes. "You might want to think about locking your door. And I'll start knocking before I just barge in."

"I don't plan on making a habit out of this kind of thing."

"Why not?" she shot back with a grin. "I would."

"Imogene Grace Prescott!" I playfully chided. "You're only fourteen! Under no circumstances should you be thinking about having sex."

"I'm not." She rolled her eyes with all the attitude of a typical teenager. Then she shrugged. "But if you like being with him, just...be with him. I can handle it. I mean, don't start making out in front of me or anything. I see enough of that in the stairwells at school. But whatever you do behind closed doors is your business. Okay?"

"Okay." I nodded, wrapping her in my arms and pressing a kiss to her head. "I love you, baby girl."

"And I love you, Mama." She sighed, nuzzling into me.

Then she lifted her eyes to mine, anxiously chewing on her bottom lip. "Can I maybe meet him now?"

I chuckled, thinking she had nothing to be nervous about. Then again, Lachlan *was* one of her all-time favorite players. Meeting him was akin to me meeting

Donnie Wahlberg during my New Kids on the Block phase.

"Sure. Then what do you say to some chocolate chip pancakes like I used to make when you were a little girl?"

She beamed. "I'd like that."

CHAPTER FOURTEEN

Lachlan

Spatula in hand, I lifted the pancake slightly, checking the color of the bottom. Seeing it had turned a brownish hue, I flipped the batch on the griddle, then cut up a few more strawberries.

After Julia went to talk to Imogene, I wanted to do something to make this situation less awkward, so I thought I'd make breakfast.

Initially, I was just going to make my usual bacon and eggs. Then I recalled Julia mentioning Imogene's favorite breakfast was chocolate chip pancakes. While I knew mine wouldn't come close to her mom's, especially considering I had to go online to find a recipe, I hoped they weren't completely inedible.

It was crazy to think how much my life had changed since meeting Julia. Cooking pancakes in the hopes of winning the approval of a fourteen-year-old girl so I could keep dating her mother?

It was a stark contrast from a few months ago when I wouldn't even entertain the notion of staying the night at a woman's place, quickly getting out of there with a promise to call mere minutes after I got off.

I never called.

Meeting Julia changed me. She brought out a side of me I thought died the night I lost Piper. Allowed me to release the guilt that had burdened me for too long now. Gave me hope.

At the sound of footsteps, I looked toward the foyer as Julia and her mini me rounded the corner. Last night, as I looked at the pictures, I'd commented on how similar they looked. But in person, it was even more remarkable. Uncanny. Sure, their hair was a different color, as were their eyes, but everything else was practically identical. Right down to their current facial expressions.

"What's going on?" Julia asked, brows scrunched.

"I hope you don't mind," I said, trying to hide my anxiety.

This was completely new territory for me. I'd never even been in a situation where I had to meet my girl-friend's parents, let alone her daughter. My last serious relationship was Piper. I was as close to her family as I was my own, even before we started dating. This current scenario was so far outside my comfort zone it was laughable.

I just hoped it didn't make Imogene uneasy to see me dressed in what was clearly my outfit from last night.

Maybe this wasn't the best idea. Maybe I should have waited until I was at least wearing clean clothes. Not a wrinkled shirt and slacks.

"I thought you might be hungry." I glanced at Imogene. "Both of you."

Imogene squinted, focusing her attention on the griddle. "Are those chocolate chip pancakes?"

I fully expected her to turn up her nose, say something to the effect that they looked nothing like her mother's. Let's face it. Compared to Julia, I was rubbish in the kitchen.

"Is that okay? I can make something else. I just—"

"Holy shit!" Imogene squealed, dropping all pretenses. "Lachlan Hale is in my kitchen making me breakfast."

"Imogene," Julia scolded. "Language."

"I'm sorry, Mama." She shifted her gaze to Julia, bouncing on her feet, obviously struggling to reel in her enthusiasm. Much like Julia often did. "But this is a swear-worthy event."

"Thanks," I offered with a slight laugh. "I think..."

"Imogene, baby," Julia continued, "I'd like you to meet Lachlan Hale. My..." She trailed off, her lips forming an adorable pout. "What are you to me? Boyfriend sounds so...inadequate."

"It certainly does. But I'll take it. It's much better than being nothing to you."

"Are you for real?" Imogene interjected, mouth agape, hand on a hip.

"Did I say something wrong?"

Suddenly, she stepped toward me, flinging her arms around my midsection. "Not in the least."

I stiffened, taken aback. I thought I'd have to work a little harder to earn her approval. I remember how suspicious I was of any man who dated my mother after my father passed away.

Then again, this was a vastly different situation. Julia didn't lose the love of her life, like my mum had. Imogene was as much a victim of Nick's actions as her mother was.

"Sorry." Imogene quickly pulled back, chewing on her lower lip as she averted her gaze. "I don't know what I was thinking. I'm a hugger. I guess I got carried away. Forgot who you were for a moment. When I heard you say that, I thought it was so stinking cute and perfect and sweet. The fact you said it to my mom made it that much better. I—"

Chuckling to myself at just how eerily alike Imogene and Julia truly were, I wrapped an arm around her, kissing the top of her head, cutting her off.

"It's okay, Imogene." I pulled back. "Or would you prefer I call you Mo?"

"Either is fine."

"Well, it's lovely to meet you, Imogene." I smiled, then glanced in Julia's direction. "And it's nice to see the apple doesn't fall too far from the tree."

"What do you mean?" Imogene tilted her head to the side at the same time as Julia, both their noses wrinkled in confusion.

I shook my head, laughing under my breath. "You both ramble when you're nervous."

"Oh." Imogene fidgeted with the hem of her shirt.

"But there's no need to be nervous around me. Or to view me as anyone other than someone who's crazy about your mum. Okay?"

"My *mum*," she chuckled, mimicking my accent.

"Yes. Your *mum*." I played up my Australian a bit.

"Now, what would you like to drink? Orange juice okay?"

"Perfect."

With a smile, I opened the refrigerator and grabbed the juice, pouring some for Imogene and placing it on the round, bistro table in the breakfast nook where I'd already arranged three place settings. Then I returned to the stove, removed the last batch of pancakes from the griddle, and added them to the plate.

"Let's eat," I announced, following Julia and Imogene to the table. I set the pancakes in the center and sat down, Julia to my right, Imogene to my left.

I watched as Imogene piled a bunch of pancakes onto her plate and covered them with syrup. As she took a large bite, all I could do was pray I hadn't fucked up the recipe.

When she closed her eyes in appreciation, I released a small breath of relief.

"Thanks for this," Julia whispered into my ear, her nearness causing a stirring deep in my belly.

I glanced her way, seeing her eyes twinkling.

In that one look, I knew she wasn't simply thanking me for making breakfast, something I tried to do for her every morning we spent together.

Her gratitude went beyond that. Went to the way I made an effort with Imogene.

I could have easily taken the out she'd given me. At my age, dating someone with a teenage daughter *was* asking a lot.

Especially since I'd spent the past five years avoiding relationships. Avoiding connecting with people in general.

If my past had taught me anything, it was that

nothing in life was perfect. We simply had to make the best out of what we had.

And I loved what I had with Julia.

CHAPTER FIFTEEN

Lachlan

"Hey," Ethan greeted as he opened the door to his loft in Midtown.

I'd been meaning to pay him a visit since I returned from Hawaii but kept putting it off. Thought with an FBI agent on the case, things would move along.

But when Ethan called over the weekend, informing me Agent Curran's hands were tied and he couldn't be a part of any sort of investigation until the FBI was officially invited in, I figured it was time to check in. See if I could do anything to help.

I doubted I could. I was a baseball player. Not an investigator.

Still, being here made me feel like I was doing *some-*

thing to get justice for Claire. For Piper. For the dozens of women whose lives had been tragically cut short by some sorry excuse of a human.

"Thanks for stopping by. I know how busy you are." He stepped back, allowing me to enter.

His condo was in an old industrial building a few blocks from Piedmont Park. I knew how high the rent in this part of town could be. The podcast must have been fairly successful to allow him to afford this place.

The far wall was all windows with a panoramic view of the city. The rest of the room was brick, the ceiling made up of industrial metal and exposed beams. It definitely suited what I'd learned about Ethan over the past few weeks.

As did how clean it was, not so much as a used coffee cup sitting in the sink.

"And you worked closely with Claire?" I mused, unable to hide my surprise as I gazed around.

Everything about this place was at complete odds with Claire's apartment.

"She was definitely a bit...disorganized." He chuckled as he ran a hand through his blond hair.

"That may just be the understatement of the year."

"She claimed she had a system." He shrugged. "What that was, I can't be sure. But it worked for her. Made her who she was."

I nodded. "Yes, it did."

A moment of silence passed between us as we remembered Claire in our own way. Then Ethan cleared his throat.

"Come on. I'll show you what I've been working on."

"Did you catch a big break yet?" I asked, half joking, half hopeful.

"I wish. But I think I'm making *some* progress with what little resources I have."

He led me into a smaller room just off the open living area, the only piece of furniture a simple metal table, four large corkboards hanging on two of the walls. The first three contained police reports, photos, and Ethan's notes. The fourth held a giant map of the United States, thumbtacks marking certain cities, a date above each.

"What's that?" I nodded toward it.

"I mapped his kills. Sometimes a visual gives you a clearer picture than just a list of places and dates."

"Did it?"

"Sure did." He walked up to the board. "Notice anything peculiar?"

"Seems like there's a concentration in this area." I gestured in the general vicinity of Georgia and South Carolina, some tacks even extending into Northern Alabama and parts of Eastern Tennessee.

"Serial killers often have a comfort zone," Ethan explained. "They don't like to stray too far from it, preferring to commit their kills where they feel most comfortable. They typically only go outside that zone if they have no choice. So, based on what we know about serial killers in general, it's reasonable to say this is his comfort zone." He circled his hand over the concentration of thumbtacks. "And if I were a gambling man, my bet is that he's from right here." He pointed to Atlanta, where there were two tacks. One with a date of March fifth five years ago. The other from a few weeks ago.

"Why? Because he killed two people in this city?"

"No. Because it's the center of what his kill radius appears to be."

"And the rest of the victims?" I looked back at the map. "There are kills as far out as Hawaii."

I pushed down the reminder I was the reason that particular girl was dead. I tried not to dwell on that, though. Instead, I found comfort in Claire's theory that, had I not been home that fateful night, this guy would have killed Piper, too.

God knows what else he would have done to her had I not intervened.

"There's one in the suburbs of LA," I continued. "One around Houston. St. Louis. Cincinnati. Hell, even as far north as Chicago and Boston."

"Those are the outliers, though." He faced me. "Even so, we can't completely discredit them. Variations from a pattern can often give us as much information, if not more, as an established pattern can."

"How?"

"Think about it." He shifted toward the corkboard again. "The majority of his kills occur within 200 miles of Atlanta."

"Yes."

"We also know this pattern is an obsession for him."

I nodded.

"Taken together, it's logical to conclude that the only reason this guy committed those kills outside of his comfort zone was because he had no choice."

"Why would that be?"

"At first, I figured maybe he was worried the cops were closing in, so he decided to travel outside his normal radius to continue the pattern. But if you look at the map, you can see he *doesn't* kill two people from the same city. At least before Claire. Which tells me two things. One, he's intentional when choosing his victims, which we pretty much assumed he was in order to repeat Jaskulski's kill cycle."

"And two?"

"I don't think Claire was his original target. I think she was killed because she was on to this guy, and he silenced her. The fact it was on July tenth was just a coincidence. Either that, or he's becoming a bit more brazen and doesn't think he'll get caught. At least not here in Atlanta."

"Okay...," I drew out.

I had no idea how Ethan figured all this out based on a bunch of thumbtacks, but what did I know?

"So Claire may not have been his original target. How do we figure out who his original target was? Have you found anything on any of your shared drives or in her files that could help?"

He snorted a laugh. "Don't I wish. I told you Claire had a system. Unfortunately, that has prevented me from figuring out what she'd been looking into the last few weeks of her life. I knew she hoped to connect these suicides to Domenic Jaskulski, but I can't figure out if she ever did. However, I do have a theory."

I arched a brow. "And that is?"

"Based on this map and what we know about serial killers, I think it's a possibility this guy travels for work and these are the locations he frequents. If we consider the 200 miles around Atlanta his main comfort zone, these other areas could possibly be secondary comfort zones. Places he visits frequently enough to be familiar with. Which would also give him an opportunity to select, observe, and attack his target. He wouldn't have the means or the confidence to pull off something like this if he didn't feel comfortable in each of these secondary locales. It doesn't fit the profile."

"So I started looking into companies with offices here in Atlanta, as well as in these outlier cities."

"An airline maybe?" I suggested. "Atlanta does have the busiest airport in the world. Houston. Los Angeles. Boston. Chicago. New York. These are all major cities where any airline would fly."

"That crossed my mind. But then I remembered something I learned when I briefly dated a flight attendant."

"What's that?"

"They often don't know where they're going from one day to the next. They certainly wouldn't be able to put in the requisite planning this guy clearly undertakes in choosing the perfect victim, then carrying out the attack. Which is why I don't believe he works for an airline. This is someone who probably has his travel schedule far enough in advance to know he'll be out of town on the date in question, requiring him to choose a victim in a different city. Hell, he may even hire a private investigator to keep tabs on them while he's back home."

"So it can be anyone," I sighed, frustrated. "We're no closer to figuring this out."

"I wouldn't say that." Ethan rolled up the sleeves of his shirt past his elbows.

For someone who worked from home, he still dressed as if there were some corporate dress code policy, wearing a button-down shirt tucked into a pair of khaki pants.

"When I noticed this pattern, I did some digging to see if my theory held merit. I ran a search of all medium and large companies with offices in Atlanta, as well as these other cities, focusing on those with a home base here."

He lifted his gaze to mine, almost hesitant.

"One company matched every single one, with one exception."

"One exception?" I asked.

He gave me a knowing look, silently telling me Piper was the exception.

I had a feeling she always would be.

"And what company matched all of this?" I asked, a premonition settling in my gut that I wasn't going to like his response.

"I think you already know the answer."

CHAPTER SIXTEEN

Lachlan

Legs seemingly on autopilot, I walked toward one of the corkboards, chest squeezing as my eyes skated over each city where I knew Julia had a location of her bakery, many of them marked with a thumbtack. My stomach knotted, a boulder lodged in my throat as my hands formed into fists.

"Are you telling me this guy works for Julia? That she may know him? That he may have unrestricted access to her right now?" With every word I spoke, my heart hammered even more.

"It's just a theory. We did bring up this possibility in Hawaii, especially once we learned the jewelry she received was not only sent to one of her bakeries using the corporate offices as a return address, but the envelopes also bore the company's logo."

I whirled around, facing him. "Which both you and Nikko said didn't mean anything! That anyone could have lifted that logo off the internet to make it appear legit. That this guy's use of the corporate address and packaging was most likely a cover or false flag."

"And that could still be the case here. This could still be someone attempting to make it appear as if this individual works for Julia."

"But it could also be someone who does?"

He paused, as if debating his answer. Then his shoulders fell. "Yes."

I squeezed my eyes shut, pinching the bridge of my nose, a tension headache starting. I shouldn't have come here today. I was due at the field in less than an hour, but my head most certainly wasn't in any place to think about baseball right now. At least I wasn't scheduled to pitch until tomorrow.

"Which is why I plan to look into this further," Ethan continued in an effort to appease me. "I have all her personnel files, including records and background checks for everyone who's ever worked for her company, from custodial staff all the way up to management. I have travel records. Flight itineraries. Receipts. If this guy does work for her, I'll find him. Trust me. He won't do anything to hurt her."

I looked up. "How do you know?"

"Because of Nick, as twisted as it may sound. She's his obsession. If this copycat...or acolyte, for lack of a better word...hopes to gain Nick's approval through this pattern of kills, he'd never consider harming a hair on Julia's head. She's protected *because* of Nick's infatuation with her."

"Protected...," I repeated, voice heavy with disbelief. Then I stormed toward one of the corkboards, yanking off the photo of Julia, beaten and bruised. I shoved it in front of his face. "She doesn't look *protected* here, Ethan."

He opened his mouth, hesitating, as if tempering the response on the tip of his tongue. "I simply said this acolyte wouldn't consider harming Julia." He gave me a knowing look.

"But Nick would," I exhaled.

"You already know the answer to that."

I pinched my eyes shut once more, a hatred I didn't think possible filling me. "How far would he go?" I asked against my better judgment.

Ethan swallowed hard, then averted his gaze, gesturing toward the corkboards. "As you already know, this guy kills his victims."

I slammed my fist down onto the desk, causing Ethan to jump. "I'm not talking about this copycat... Acolyte... Whatever the bloody hell he is! I'm talking about Nick. How far would he go? Based on everything you've learned about him, how far would he take things with Julia?"

"He's in prison," Ethan reminded me calmly. "Serving a life sentence. He'll never see the light of day again."

"Just. Tell. Me," I demanded through clenched teeth. When he didn't respond, I choked out, "Please. I just... I need to know."

Silence filled the room as he stared at me, the only sound that of the ticking of a clock and the faint noise of Atlanta traffic on the streets below.

Finally, he sighed. "She's his Hera."

I blinked, confused. "His... His what?"

"He fancied himself Zeus. The god of gods from Greek Mythology."

"You're going to have to be more specific. I didn't pay attention in my literature classes whenever we read any of that stuff."

"Basically, Zeus was a giant narcissist. Thought he should be able to put his dick into any being, mortal or immortal. But God help anyone who so much as looked at Hera the wrong way." He shrugged. "The same goes for Nick and Julia. Their relationship was never based on love, despite what he made her believe to win her over. Instead, it was based on obsession."

"And this obsession... How far would he take it?"

"As far as necessary."

"Would he..." I stopped, swallowing hard, summoning the strength to ask the question I needed the answer to.

The question I feared I already knew the answer to.

"Would he kill her?"

Ethan slowly brought his gaze to mine. He didn't have to utter a single syllable. His response was written all over his face.

"I believe he would."

I released a shuttering breath, my throat closing up.

"But you don't have to worry about him. Like I said, he's locked up. Spending the rest of his life behind bars. Julia's safe."

I wished I could find comfort in Ethan's assurances. I couldn't, though. Not until that fucker was dead.

Only then would I be certain she was safe.

A chiming cut through the tense atmosphere.

"Sorry," Ethan said as he reached into his pocket and pulled out his cell. "It's Agent Curran. I should take this. Might be important."

I nodded. While Ethan slipped out of the room, I stepped toward the corkboards once again.

As I perused all the research Ethan had done, all of it obviously important enough to keep readily accessible, I came to a stop in front of Julia's victim statement, a sticky note with Ethan's familiar scrawl on top of it.

- *Multiple incidents of forced intercourse.*
- *Psychological abuse throughout marriage.*
- *Threatened to take daughter from her.*

My jaw clenched, hands fisting. I knew this guy was a bastard who didn't deserve the air he breathed. Knew he'd hurt Julia, in addition to several other women. But seeing it broken down into three concise bullet points filled me with a sort of protectiveness I'd never felt before. And it wasn't just for Julia. But also Imogene. If that monster so much as attempted to come near either of them, I wouldn't hesitate to end his life.

"Hey."

At the sound of Ethan's voice, I faced him. "What did Curran want?"

Ethan parted his lips, obviously uneasy.

"If it has something to do with Claire, I have a right to know. She's my sister."

He studied me for a moment, then sighed. "There's not much Curran can do right now, as you know. Nonetheless, he still has some privileges as a federal agent. Like requesting inmate visitation records, as well as incoming and outgoing mail logs, in order to ensure victim safety."

This certainly piqued my interest. "You mean—"

"Curran pulled Domenic Jaskulski's visitation records and mail logs for the past five years. Truthfully, he didn't think he'd uncover much. Most of his mail was from fans. Women declaring their love for him, as twisted as that sounds. As far as visitors, he didn't get many. He has had routine visits from a prison outreach ministry, but that isn't what struck Curran as odd, although he does intend on looking into this group."

"Then what *did* strike him as odd?"

He chewed on his bottom lip, shifting from foot to foot. "Over the past two months, he was permitted twelve media visits, all by the same person."

I uncrossed my arms, pulse increasing. "Media visits?"

"The First Amendment allows the media access to prison inmates, contingent on the warden agreeing. Each prison has different requirements, but typically, if there's a compelling reason and the reporter has a clean record, they're granted access."

"And what reporter was granted access to Domenic Jaskulski?" I asked, although I had a feeling I already knew the answer.

"Claire."

My hands clenched, ears pounding, fire scalding my veins. It took everything in me to resist the urge to punch the wall. Instead, I advanced on Ethan, who backed up, holding his hands up defensively in front of his body.

"Why? What did she want to talk to him about?"

"That's what Curran hoped I could tell him, but I

can't. She never told me about this. It's like..." He trailed off, shaking his head. "It's like I'm learning about a completely different side of Claire."

I relaxed my stance, knowing all too well what that felt like.

"All I know is what Curran told me. Over the past two months, she was granted access to Jaskulski on multiple occasions... Including the day before she died."

CHAPTER SEVENTEEN

Julia

"Look who's back from her little sex-cation," Naomi remarked as I entered my company's corporate office in Downtown Atlanta later that morning.

Much later than I typically showed up for work.

The place buzzed with energy, dozens of people smiling at me before returning to whatever they did to keep my company running. Payroll. Purchasing. Merchandising.

All things I never thought I'd have to worry about on such a large scale.

Yet here we were.

There was a time when, had I attempted to take off

three weeks from work, my business would have come to a grinding halt.

Hell, there was a time that would have happened had I missed a single day.

Not anymore. Everything continued without me. It made me wonder if I were needed here at all, apart from being the face of the company.

Made me feel like nothing more than a glorified spokesperson. Not someone who put her blood, sweat, and tears into building this company from scratch.

"It was *not* a sex-cation," I muttered to Naomi with a roll of my eyes.

Even though the past few weeks with Lachlan kind of was.

Since returning from Hawaii, I practically lived at his place. I even took extra time away from the office, which allowed me to spend the mornings and early after-noons with him before he had to head to the ballpark for pre-game warmups. When he got home, he crawled into bed and made love to me until we were both too exhausted to stay awake another second.

It was...paradise.

"Whatever you say," Naomi chided, following me into my corner office, Atlanta buzzing outside the floor-to-ceiling windows.

"I want to hear everything." She plopped down into

the chair across from my desk. "And don't leave out a single, juicy detail."

"I already told you everything." I shrugged dismissively as I sat behind my desk and pulled my laptop out of my bag. "We're trying to make something work."

"And how's that going?"

"Good."

"*Good*? That's all you're going to give me? I want details. What have you been doing? Besides fucking all hours of the day. Have you gone to—"

"Excuse me, Ms. Prescott."

I flung my gaze to the open door of my office, my assistant, Rina, standing there, a cup of coffee in her hands.

"Come on in, Rina."

"I hope you had a nice time away." She set the mug in front of me.

"Did she ever," Naomi shot back under her breath.

I glared at my friend before plastering a smile onto my face. "It was exactly what I needed. Is there anything on my schedule today?"

She looked down at her tablet. "There's a director's meeting at noon. Your agent has also requested a meeting to discuss a few offers that have come in. I told her you'd be back today and I'd see if you could meet with her. Is this afternoon okay?"

"Sure," I answered, feigning enthusiasm.

I missed the days my time was spent in a kitchen, covered in flour, interacting with customers, watching their expressions as they took their first bite of whatever concoction I'd whipped up that day. Now they were filled with investor meetings, reviewing sales figures, sitting through advertising pitches, and listening to arguments about where to expand to next.

"I'll let her know." Rina made a note on her tablet. "Is there anything else you need right now?"

"No. Thank you."

"Of course." With a smile, she turned, making her way out of my office.

Once we were alone, I pinned Naomi with a glare. "Try to refrain from letting the entire office know about my personal life." I lowered my voice. "No one can know about Lachlan right now."

"But I thought you guys were together."

I smoothed a hand down my dress. "And we are."

"Then what's the problem?"

"He's not someone I can just...be with. Not with who he is. I have to consider Imogene. And the way the media will respond to news of baseball's most eligible bachelor not only being in a relationship, but with an older woman who has a daughter."

"It's not like he's Jason Momoa. Or Brad Pitt. It might be news for a day before being pushed out of everyone's mind. If it makes headlines at all."

I closed my eyes, drawing in a deep breath, not wanting to admit she was right. Lachlan *wasn't* like Jason Momoa or Brad Pitt. Or even Tom Brady. While he was certainly a legend in baseball circles, especially in Atlanta, if you weren't a fan, most people probably wouldn't recognize him or had even heard of him.

"Unless there's another reason." She arched a brow. "Unless your reluctance isn't about the world learning of your relationship, but one person in particular."

I squared my shoulders. "I have to be careful."

"So it *is* because of Nick."

"I—"

"Julia," she interjected, sitting forward in the chair, "he's in prison. He can't get to you anymore."

"I know that."

But just because he was in prison didn't mean he couldn't get to me anymore. Not after recent events.

Recent events I hadn't shared with Naomi.

"Then why are you still letting him control you?"

"I'm not," I argued. "I'm in a relationship again."

She pushed out a disbelieving laugh. "I don't think you are."

"What makes you say that?"

"What do you and Lachlan do together?"

I parted my lips, but before I could respond, she interrupted.

"Things that don't involve sex."

I snapped my mouth shut. While we've done *some* things outside of the bedroom, like lounged by his gorgeous pool or relaxed in his theater room, it all eventually led to sex.

"Listen, Jules," she began, voice soothing, "I get I'm the last person you should take relationship advice from, considering I don't have a great track record. But when I was with someone, I was *with* them. Not just in secret. Not just on a superficial level.

"If you're going to be with Lachlan, you need to be with him in every aspect of your life. You need to let him *in* to every aspect of your life. He may be understanding right now, since it's still new and there are complications here most relationships don't have to deal with. But at some point, you're going to have to finally jump. Because, right now, it appears as if your feet are in the same place they've always been. Allowing Nick to manipulate you, even from behind bars."

"Naomi...," I sighed, searching my brain for the words to explain why this was best for all involved. At least for now.

Maybe if she knew the truth, that there was a very strong possibility Nick was connected to over a dozen recent murders masked as suicide, including Lachlan's own sister, she'd understand *why* I needed to keep this quiet. I hated the idea of Lachlan becoming a target because of me. And that was precisely what would happen.

"There's something I—"

A loud commotion came from within the outer office.

Naomi turned around in the chair as I stood, looking into the cubicle-filled space. When my eyes fell on the source of it, I sucked in a breath, pulse spiking as dread settled deep in my stomach.

"Sir," Rina cautioned in a feeble attempt to run interference, jumping in front of my open office door. "You can't go in there without an appointment."

"I don't need one."

Before I had a chance to do any sort of damage control, Lachlan burst into my office, stalking toward me. He pulled my body to his, clinging onto me tighter than he ever has.

I stiffened, taken aback by not only the fact he was in my office, but that he was hugging me, the door wide open, allowing anyone to witness.

To gossip.

To talk.

I couldn't have that.

I quickly pushed out of his hold, putting as much distance between us as possible.

"Mr. Hale." I gritted out a smile, pushing my hair

behind my ears. "To what do I owe this...unexpected visit?"

He stared at me for a beat, brows furrowed, obviously confused by the formality in my tone.

What choice did I have? We'd agreed to keep this relationship quiet. For now. He couldn't expect me to just start making out with him in my office, in view of my employees.

Even if we were openly dating, I still wouldn't engage in public displays of affection in my place of business.

"I need to talk to you," he finally said, a gravity in his tone. "It's important."

"I'm sorry, Ms. Prescott." Rina's gaze ping-ponged between Lachlan and me. "Do you need me to call security?"

I shifted my attention to the petite blonde. "That won't be necessary. Mr. Hale is a friend."

"Friend," Naomi snorted under her breath.

"Just give us a moment, please, Rina."

"Of course." She glanced Lachlan's way, a subtle blush blooming on her cheeks, then disappeared from my office.

"That means you, too," I said to Naomi before dropping my voice. "And not a word about this to anyone. I'm sure there are already rumors spreading like wildfire. I need them stopped. And quickly."

"Of course. I wouldn't want anyone to think you were happy."

"That's not—"

"Yes. It is." She pinned me with a stare, then spun, closing the door behind her.

CHAPTER EIGHTEEN

Julia

Closing my eyes, I took a calming breath, wishing I could get a do-over of this day.

First, Imogene walked in on Lachlan and me having sex.

Then Naomi refused to understand why I needed to keep this thing with Lachlan quiet for the time being.

Then, the icing on the cake, Lachlan barged into my office and hugged me for all to see, no doubt causing the rumor mill to spring to life.

What else could possibly go wrong?

"You can't do this, Lachlan," I declared in a firm voice, glaring at him. "You can't just burst into my office and...and...hug me!"

"Friends hug," he said with a hint of venom, throwing my words back at me.

"I told you why things needed to be this way." I stepped toward him, softening my expression. "I need time. Please be patient."

"And I told you I would be. That I understood your reasoning."

"Then why did you come here? If you—"

"Because I tried calling and you didn't answer, Julia." The muscles in his face clenched, eyes awash with concern. "Texted, too. No response. All I could think was that..." He swallowed, the cords in his neck throbbing.

I covered his chest with my hand. "What?"

My heart ached at the vulnerability covering every inch of him. A stark contrast from the man I met mere weeks ago. A man who masked his true feelings with anger.

He wrapped his arms around me, exhaling deeply. I didn't fight him. Not now that we were behind closed doors.

Then again, the fact my office door was closed, something I never did, probably only increased everyone's curiosity. It wouldn't take a genius to put two and two together. Everyone who followed sports knew he was from Hawaii. I'd just opened a bakery on the same island where he spent his teenage years. Upon my return, I took an unprecedented two-week break from work, only for Lachlan Hale to appear and hug me in front of the entire office on my first day back.

I could only imagine the chatter currently going on around the proverbial water cooler.

But when Lachlan brought his hands to my face, I didn't care about that. All I did care about was him and what caused him such panic. And that was precisely what I saw when I peered into his vibrant, blue eyes.

Anxiety.

Trepidation.

Fear.

"I was so scared that something had happened to you."

Sighing, I placed my hand on his cheek, offering him what little comfort I could give.

I understood his concern. He'd just lost his sister on the fifth anniversary of Piper's death. With the likelihood Nick was somehow connected to both Claire's and Piper's deaths, it was no wonder he worried about me, too.

In the aftermath of Nick's attack on me and subsequent arrest, I'd suffered from severe anxiety. Didn't want to let any of my loved ones out of my sight for fear Nick would somehow get to them.

In a way, I still struggled with it, although on a lesser scale.

Regardless, there were still times all it took was one thing for that anxiety to go into overdrive. A memory. A smell. A word. The fear would claw at me, making it nearly impossible to breathe. To think.

To live.

Lachlan must have suffered the same thing after *his* loss.

"I'm fine," I assured him. "I'm safe here."

"Are you, though?" His voice rose in pitch toward the end.

"What are you talking about?"

He stared at me for a moment, then said, "I went to see Ethan."

I stepped out of his hold. "Did he find anything?"

"Nothing concrete. But he did discover something...interesting."

He pulled his phone out of his pocket. After tapping at it, he handed it to me. I squinted at the screen, trying to figure out what I was looking at.

"It's a map of this guy's kills," Lachlan explained. "Ethan thought a visual might help."

"Did it?"

He nodded slowly. "Do you know what he learned?"

I looked at the map again. "That this guy is probably

from this area of the country, since his victims seem to be concentrated here?"

"Yes. But that's not all. He came up with a theory to explain the kills that occurred outside of this area. And do you know what that is?"

I remained silent, staring at the map, each of the thumbtacks located near major cities.

Major cities where I had a bakery.

"This person *is* from this area, but probably travels for work to these other cities, and routinely enough to stalk a potential victim, learn everything he needs about them, then plan his attack. So Ethan investigated companies located in Atlanta, ones that also had branches in or around these other cities. Do you know what company popped up over and over again?"

"The Mad Batter," I exhaled.

This shouldn't have come as a surprise. After all, each piece of jewelry I'd received came in packaging bearing the company's logo and my corporate office's return address.

Even so, Nikko, Agent Curran, and Ethan weren't entirely convinced this person was actually connected to my company. Thought it was just a smoke screen, considering anyone could have easily lifted my logo off the internet and designed a replica of the packaging we use.

Now I feared all the background checks I'd insisted

be conducted on every single employee — whether a high-ranking member of my corporate team or an hourly worker — hadn't been as effective as I'd hoped.

It also made me question whether the employee records I'd handed over to Agent Curran and Ethan would be useful. I feared whoever was behind this would always remain two steps ahead of us.

Ahead of me.

"Yes, Julia." Lachlan's lower lip quivered. "This guy could be in this fucking building right now. So I'm sorry I came here when you made it quite clear you didn't want to be seen in public with me. At least not yet. But when I called and you didn't answer..."

His voice caught. He took a deep breath, briefly looking away before returning his eyes to mine, cupping my face in a tight hold.

"All I could think was something had happened to you. I know it's crazy. That the likelihood of anything happening in a building filled with people is so minuscule it's absurd. Not to mention the security you have in place here...even though I was able to get through with no problem."

"Probably because you're Lachlan Hale. Not sure anyone wants to mess with you after you landed that cop in the hospital," I joked in an attempt to lighten the tension.

But I knew he wouldn't allow me to escape this

discussion. Wouldn't let me downplay the very real possibility that this threat was even closer to home than we originally thought.

"I didn't do enough when Claire voiced her concerns," Lachlan continued, pain and passion filling every single syllable, "and she lost her life because of it. I won't do that to you." Grip on my face tightening, his lips slowly descended to mine. "I can't lose you, too."

"You won't lose me," I murmured against his mouth. "Promise."

It wasn't a promise anyone could truly hope to keep.

Regardless, Lachlan managed to find peace in my reassurance, the tension in his body melting away as he moved his lips against mine, coaxing them to part. This was definitely inappropriate. Not to mention risky.

But from the beginning, I'd been completely power-less to resist this man.

And I was still just as powerless.

I opened for him, our tongues tangling in a sweet kiss. Then he groaned, deepening the exchange. His motions became more desperate. More needy. More wanton.

A tiny whimper escaped my throat as his hand roamed my frame, squeezing my breast through my dress. This was so wrong, but the feeling of his hands on my body was my undoing, erasing every single thought in my mind.

Except for how this man made me feel.

Cherished.

Revered.

Alive.

I'd never felt so alive in my life. So ready to drop all my inhibitions and just live in the moment with Lachlan, to hell with what the future held.

To hell with any potential ramifications.

Panting, he tore his lips from mine, burying his head in the crook of my neck. I savored in the roughness of his skin against mine as his hand skimmed down my body, grabbing my thigh and hooking my leg around his waist.

"Lachlan..." His name was a cross between a mewl and a warning, my rationale returning for a brief moment.

I wanted to keep our relationship quiet for a reason.

Making out in my office certainly wouldn't keep it quiet.

Although I had a feeling we were about to do way more than just make out.

"Don't tell me to stop," he pleaded, voice dripping with desperation.

This was so much more than just him wanting to get off. The way he begged made me think he physically needed the reminder I was still here. That we would get through whatever the hell was going on.

So, instead of doing what every voice inside my head

insisted I should, I brought my lips to his neck, kissing him gently.

"Lachlan... Don't stop."

With an animalistic growl, he hooked his fingers into my panties and pushed them down my legs. I stepped out of them, chest heaving, body tingling with anticipation. In one quick motion, he lifted me up and slammed my back against the wall. It caused a loud thump to reverberate in the space, a few of the photos crashing to the floor.

I looked their way, worried the sound would cause someone to come check on me. But before I could give it too much thought, he pulled his arousal out of his shorts and thrust inside me, covering my mouth with his to swallow my cries of pleasure.

What we were doing was risky, especially with the growing possibility that someone who worked for me was somehow involved in these recent deaths.

Was possibly working with Nick.

But I didn't care about that right now. Nothing seemed to bother me when Lachlan was near. The way he made me feel blinded me to everything else.

He was like a drug. Something I kept returning to so I could experience a brief moment of bliss.

Of happiness.

Even if it ended up killing us both.

My body craving release from my earlier stolen

orgasm, it took no time at all for Lachlan to push me to the peak, my muscles tightening, heart racing.

"You like this, don't you?" he grunted, his motions becoming more and more punishing with every mind-numbing thrust. "Like that I'm fucking you in your office."

"Oh god," I moaned, closing my eyes as I fought to prolong the ecstasy overwhelming me.

He wrapped his hand around my throat, making me fling my eyes back to his. "Say it, Julia. Tell me you like it when I fuck you in your office like this. That you like knowing anyone could walk in on me drilling you."

"I don't like it," I panted, struggling to capture a breath.

He paused, arching a brow.

I leaned toward him, nibbling on his bottom lip. "I fucking *love* it."

Growling, he tightened his hold on my ass and carried me the few steps to my desk, placing me onto it, my back flush with the surface. He hooked my legs over his shoulders, his pupils dilating as he peered down at me splayed out before him, completely at his mercy.

I was breaking every rule in my book right now.

But nothing had ever felt so right.

"Please, Lachlan... Make me come."

Nostrils flaring, he drove into me with fever and desperation, each thrust harder and more punishing than the last. When he pressed his thumb against my clit, I detonated around him. Forgetting where I was, I cried out. He covered my mouth with his hand, his motions growing more frenzied until he stilled, then jerked through his own release, collapsing on top of me.

Neither of us moved for several moments, the sound of our breathing filling my office, the only other noises that of a typical office setting — phones ringing, fingers tapping on keyboards, people talking.

"I'm sorry," Lachlan said.

"For what? Fucking me?" I waggled my brows.

He laughed slightly. "I'll never apologize for that." He circled his hips. I could have sworn I felt his erection spring back to life. This man was a machine. "You feel too good to ever be sorry about being inside you."

"The feeling's mutual." I wrapped my legs around his waist, teasing him.

He groaned, kissing me, tongue swiping mine. Then he stepped back and adjusted himself, rebuttoning his pants.

Grabbing a pile of tissues, he cleaned me up and helped me to my feet, holding my panties out before stowing them in his pocket with a smirk.

"Fiend."

"Maybe." He winked, running his hands down my arms. "But I *am* sorry for bursting in here. I get why you want things to stay quiet for now. Just please promise me

I don't have to keep this a secret forever. That's all I ask, Julia. That someday I can tell the world how bloody amazing you are."

My heart expanded in my chest, the way this man so easily bared his soul to me invigorating. A breath of fresh air after a lifetime of repression.

I rested my hand against his cheek. "I promise. I just... I need some time. Make sure Imogene fully understands what it means for me to date someone like you. I'm not quite sure she can see the reality through the cloud of excitement just yet."

"I promise I will do everything I can to protect—" He stopped short.

It didn't matter. I knew what he was going to say. That he'd do everything in his power to protect me. To protect Imogene.

"This," he continued. "I will do everything I can to protect this. To protect what we have." He treated me to that smile that both melted my heart and jumpstarted it at the same time. "And I promise to never barge into your office again."

I gave him a coy look. "Well, I wouldn't say *never*." I bit my lower lip.

"Oh, no?" His eyes darkened as he curved toward me, lips a breath from mine. "Why's that?"

"There are some...benefits to having you here."

"Well then..." His mouth skimmed mine. "Just call,

and I'll happily barge in again." He sensually rocked his hips against me. "And again. And again."

I ran my hands through his hair. "You're going to make me break all my rules, aren't you?"

"Rules are made to be broken, love."

CHAPTER NINETEEN

Agent Curran

The stench of shit, urine, and something unique to every prison Agent John Curran had ever stepped foot into permeated the corridor as an officer led him toward an interrogation room. He knew he was taking a risk in doing this, fully aware it might raise a few red flags with his superiors at the Bureau.

But it had been almost a month since he'd learned Claire Hale had visited Domenic Jaskulski in prison. Despite Ethan Shore combing through all her files, he'd yet to find anything about why she made a dozen visits to this prison, spending an hour with this man each time.

He may have been barking up the wrong tree, but he couldn't ignore the feeling in his gut that Claire's death and her visits with Domenic Jaskulski were somehow connected.

So, while Ethan tried to uncover what that connection could be, John Curran used the limited resources he *did* have. As a federal agent, it was well within his rights to visit an offender in one of his previous cases. Ensure the victims he was still incarcerated. That he wasn't committing any new crimes. That their lives weren't in danger.

That was all this visit was. Simply a run-of-the-mill check-in with a notorious serial stalker, rapist, and murderer.

Nothing more.

The officer stopped outside a metal door and pressed his thumb against the scanner. The door buzzed, and the officer held it open, allowing Agent Curran to enter the interrogation room, nothing but a table and two chairs sitting in the middle of the stark space.

Sitting in one of those chairs, his wrists cuffed and chained to a bar in the center of the table, was a man he helped put behind bars years ago.

A man he'd hoped would have received a state-mandated needle in his arm.

Sadly, the jury didn't believe the prosecution met its burden in proving Domenic Jaskulski acted with the required intent to convict him of murder.

Instead, he was now serving a life sentence for rape,

aggravated assault, manslaughter, and a slew of other charges.

But not murder.

"Agent Curran," Domenic crooned in a refined, Southern drawl that had always sent shivers down his spine. It was class and intelligence personified, yet also contained a hint of something else.

Something malicious.

John glanced behind him, giving the officer a nod. When the door closed, leaving them alone, he refocused his attention on the prisoner.

"Mr. Jaskulski," John replied respectfully in the hopes it would encourage his cooperation.

"To what do I owe this visit?" Domenic's lips curved up at the corners. "I would call it unexpected, but it's not. In truth, I thought you'd come by much sooner. It's almost September."

John lowered himself to the chair, placing a folder onto the table. Then he slid a hardcover book toward Domenic.

"What's this?" he asked, brow raised.

"I heard you've been asking the library for this, but they've refused your request. I pulled a few strings."

Domenic picked up the book, opening it to the first page, a smile pulling on his arguably attractive face.

His sandy blond hair showed some signs of aging,

lighter and thinner, his face having more wrinkles than during his lengthy trial.

Regardless, no one could argue he wasn't a good-looking man.

Which probably explained the piles of fan mail he still received from women obsessed with true crime podcasts and documentaries.

John would never understand how anyone could idolize a criminal, especially one who murdered women.

"*The Count of Monte Cristo*," Domenic read as his eyes skated over the title page. "A wonderful story about a man who was wrongfully imprisoned finally seeking revenge upon those who stole everything from him."

"Is it a story of revenge, though?" John asked.

Domenic's eyes lit up over the prospect of being able to hold some sort of intelligent conversation with another person, something John knew he typically wasn't able to do.

"What do you think the moral of dear Edmond Dantès' story is then, Special Agent Curran?"

"Redemption. Initially, he may have wanted those who betrayed him to pay for their misdeeds. In the end, though, he realized only one being can play God."

"'*L'humaine sagesse était tout entière dans ces deux mots: attendre et espérer*,'" Domenic recited with perfect French enunciation. "'All human wisdom is contained in these two words—'"

"'Wait and hope,'" John finished, familiar with the famous last line of the book.

"Wait and hope."

He held John's gaze for a moment, then cleared his throat. "Now, what can I do for you today? I can only assume you didn't come all the way out here to give me a book and discuss which of the myriad of themes present in Dumas' writing is the more important one."

"You're right." John squared his shoulders, steeling himself for the battle of wits he was certain was about to be unleashed.

After nearly thirty years as a federal agent, he'd confronted more criminals than he could possibly count.

But Domenic Jaskulski was the only one who'd ever gotten under his skin. And not just because of his personal connection to Jaskulski's crimes. It went deeper than that.

Opening the folder, John pushed a photo toward Domenic, carefully studying his reaction. He knew this man wouldn't voluntarily give him the information he was after.

But there was a lot John could pick up from his body language.

And as Domenic's eyes went to the image of Claire Hale in the bathtub, body submerged in water, an arm dangling over the side, blood staining the tile below, his body language made his excitement clear. Pupils dilated, jaw twitched, breathing increased.

"She's beautiful," he remarked, almost in awe.

"She's dead," John snipped back.

"Do you not find beauty in death, Agent Curran?"

"Not exactly."

"You see, that's your problem." He folded his hands, his handcuffs clanging against the metal table. "That's the majority of society's problem. You all look at death as this horrible occurrence instead of appreciating it for the gift it is."

John barked out a disbelieving laugh. "You think death is a gift?"

"An end to suffering? Absolutely."

"You mean an end to life."

"No...," Domenic drew out. "I mean an end to suffering. Not everyone leads a happy life, Agent Curran. Not everyone *wants* to live. For some people, living is a form of torture." He paused, lips curving into a sly smile, causing the hairs on the back of John's nape to stand on end. "Take your dear niece, Annabelle, for instance."

"What about Annabelle?" John asked through a clenched jaw, hands fisting.

It took every ounce of restraint he possessed to resist the temptation to break every tooth in Domenic's charming smile. He didn't deserve to so much as think of Annabelle, let alone say her name.

Domenic leaned toward him as much as the cuffs would allow. "Do you honestly think she was happy? Her father dies... That would be your brother," he added with a hint of superiority.

"I'm aware."

"Then, when she's a very impressionable and beautiful young teenager, her mom remarries."

"A teacher. And church deacon. A good man."

"Oh, come now, Agent Curran. I thought you were smarter than that. You saw me for who I was before anyone else did. Surely you saw the same in the man who took your brother's place."

"What are you suggesting?" John asked as evenly as possible, fighting to suppress his emotions. That was what Domenic wanted. What he got off on.

John refused to give in.

"You know exactly what I'm suggesting." His dark eyes bore into John's, not a single hint of deception within. "The same thing I'm sure you perhaps questioned yourself on the rare occasion you took a break from this obsession you have with your career and spent some time with your niece. You must have noticed how uneasy she became whenever her dear old stepdad was around." His lips curled into a sneer, voice becoming more malevolent. "Whenever he would touch her. And he touched her a lot, didn't he?"

John's nostrils flared, his anger building with every

second he spent listening to this disgusting excuse for a human speak of his niece.

But he wasn't so much angry at Domenic as he was at himself.

Because, as much as he didn't want to admit it, the man was right.

Annabelle's stepfather *did* touch her a lot. She *did* get uneasy around him. John thought it was due to him taking her father's place. The result of a typical teenage girl's attitude.

"It's no wonder he always dragged her on those homebuilding missions," Domenic continued. "Unrestricted access to her without her mother being the wiser? Or maybe she knew what he was doing, yet didn't care since she needed someone to help support her and her daughters."

He tilted his head. "Tell me, Agent Curran. How's…" His brows furrowed. "Oh, what's her name? Gretchen? Annabelle's younger sister? The baby her mother was pregnant with when your brother was killed in the line of duty. She was quite young when Annabelle passed away, so she'd be…" A mischievous grin pulled on his face, his eyes dancing with amusement. "Well, she'd be a teenager now, wouldn't she? I do hope it's not too late."

"You bastard," John hissed out through his clenched jaw, the words escaping before he could stop them.

Domenic raised his hands in front of him. "*I'm* not the one who raped her."

"That's not what your journals said. According to those, you *did* rape Annabelle. You drugged her, broke into her apartment, then raped her."

"I admitted no such thing. Not once did I say I raped her."

"That's right. You 'freed' her," John mimicked, using air quotes.

"Precisely. I gave her what she needed to finally have the courage to end her suffering." Domenic nodded toward the photograph of Claire Hale. "Just like this beautiful woman ended her suffering."

John lifted his brows. He hadn't mentioned how Claire had died. Hadn't mentioned anything about her at all.

"Did she?"

"It appears so. Wrists slit. Submerged in a bathtub. Tile stained with blood." He pushed the photo back across the table, but John could sense it was a struggle, Domenic continually glancing at it. "It is a bit gory for my taste."

"Her name is Claire Hale."

"I heard all about her tragic death, but I'm not quite sure why the FBI's interested in a suicide. Correct me if I'm wrong, but according to the local newspaper, suicide *was* the final determination of the investigation. Was it not?"

"It was."

"But you don't believe that to be the case?"

"I don't."

"And do the fine, upstanding individuals at Major Crimes here in Atlanta concur with you? Or is there not much physical evidence to support your theory? If I'm right, which I usually am, the FBI doesn't have jurisdiction to investigate local crimes. Not unless they're invited in by local officials. And since I haven't heard a thing about them reopening their investigation into Ms. Hale's death, I'm guessing you haven't been, making this more of a personal matter. Correct?"

John nodded. "Correct."

He'd probably get in deep shit if his superiors found out he was here at all, even if he claimed he was simply checking on an inmate on behalf of a victim. Routine offender checks didn't typically involve sitting down for a conversation. But the warden was a good friend who happily consented to John's request, agreeing to keep it between the two of them, as long as nothing went awry.

"And how do you expect *me* to help you?" Domenic ran his finger along Claire's face, a creepy sort of appreciation on his expression.

"I know she visited you on multiple occasions over the past few months, including the day before she died."

"You think *I* had something to do with her death? She took her own life, Agent Curran. Not to mention..." He lifted his chained hands, the sound reverberating in the room. "I've been a bit preoccupied lately. Not much time for leisure, I'm afraid."

"You're right. There's no way you'd be involved. That would take a level of planning by a criminal mastermind no one could possibly pull off, especially in here." John waved a hand at his surroundings.

He didn't believe the veracity of his statement for a second. Instead, he said it purely to get a reaction. And he certainly got one. Domenic's expression turned indignant. He held his head high, spine stiff, as if the insinuation he wasn't intelligent enough to commit crimes while incarcerated was a slap in the face.

It was all John needed to confirm his suspicion that Domenic was somehow involved in these more recent deaths.

Or, at the very least, was definitely aware of them.

"But I'm not here to question you about Claire's death, since I know you're not even remotely involved. I wanted to talk to you about what you and Claire discussed during her visits."

"I don't see how our conversations could be of any help."

"Sometimes it's the smallest thing that helps crack a case. So anything you can tell me about your visits with

Claire could be useful. Her behavior. Demeanor. What you discussed. Anyone else who may have been aware of her time with you." He raised a brow. "It's my understanding you've amassed quite a following of female fans, many of whom would probably love to be able to spend the time with you Claire was allowed. Perhaps this was the work of one of them. Trying to get your attention by committing a crime similar to what you once did."

Domenic studied John for a beat, seeming to consider his request. Then he relaxed his posture. "Okay, Special Agent. I'm willing to help you. I'll happily share everything I learned about Claire Hale over our rather enlightening visits. But in exchange, I need *you* to help *me*."

"You're serving a life sentence without the possibility of early release. I can't do anything to change that. This isn't an official visit anyway. Just an...informal inquiry. I don't have many strings available to pull, so to speak."

"That's true." That same, conniving smile curled Domenic's mouth once more. "But I do believe you have at least one string you can pull... So to speak."

"What's that?"

Domenic leaned across the table, eyes cold, expression hard. "I want to see my wife."

CHAPTER TWENTY

Julia

"One four." Wes placed a card face-down on the patio table, his expression even.

I swept my gaze over him, more than aware of all his tells. But nothing about his demeanor indicated he was lying.

At least I didn't think it did.

"Two fives," Imogene said after a beat, adding her own card to the top of the growing pile.

Everyone glanced around the table as we gauged each other very carefully. With every card added to the top, the risk grew.

As did the potential reward.

"Six to you, little man," Wes said, beaming at his son.

Eli struggled a bit with his cards, his hands not as big as ours, making it difficult for him to hold them all without dropping them. Imogene leaned over and whispered something into his ear, as she always did when we played this game. Smiling up at his older cousin, Eli pulled a card from his hand and added it.

"One six." Then he looked up at the man sitting on the other side of him.

A man who, over the past few weeks, had become such a huge part of my day-to-day life, even when we weren't physically together.

While Lachlan and I continued to keep our relationship a secret from the public, I still included him in every aspect of my private life.

My family life.

Since introducing him to Wes, Londyn, and Eli, he'd become a fixture during our family get-togethers, as if he'd always been here. Like he belonged here.

And in my heart, I felt he did.

Which was why I should have just taken the final leap and gone public with our relationship, consequences be damned. A part of me wanted to. But after living all my life in survival mode, it wasn't so easy for me to flip the switch.

There were times I could tell it frustrated Lachlan. He'd repeatedly asked me to have Wes watch Imogene so I could get away for some of his road games, especially as the season went on and the games became more and more important.

But every time, I turned him down.

He took it in stride, though. Understood my reluctance. Not only because of the attention that could fall on Imogene and me, but also because of all the uncertainty regarding Ethan's investigation, which had all but ground to a halt over the past several weeks. He was still digging, still hoping to find some tiny piece of evidence that could help figure out who could be behind all of this.

But every promising piece of information turned out to be a dead end.

And October thirteenth was now just two weeks away.

"I guess it's my turn then."

Lachlan's voice pulled me from my thoughts, my skin warming at the sound.

I brought my gaze to his, fighting to hide my smile when his eyes briefly met mine before returning to his cards. I studied him, trying to determine if he were about to bullshit all of us about his cards. Knowing him as intimately as I did, you'd think I'd recognize his tells.

So far, I didn't.

Neither did anyone else.

He'd officially taken over Naomi's place of honor as the Queen of Bullshit. Or Queen of Bull, as we tried to

call her around the kids, something we constantly struggled with.

Which was probably why Imogene loved playing
this game. Her swear jar typically overflowed with dollar
bills afterward.

"Sevens to me," Lachlan mused, gaze skating over his
hand. Then he placed his remaining cards face-down on
top of the pile. "Three sevens."

"Bullshit," I immediately stated.

What did I have to lose? If I were wrong, the game
was over anyway.

But if I were right, Lachlan would have to pick up all
the cards.

God, I hoped I was right.

"That's a dollar," Imogene sang.

Rolling my eyes, I reached into my back pocket,
peeling off another dollar bill and adding it to the pile
she'd amassed throughout the game. Then I returned my
attention to Lachlan, relaxing back in my chair, the
September sun warming my skin as we sat on the back
patio.

There was no telling how many more nice days we'd
have now that fall was right around the corner. So I was
going to enjoy it while I could.

And today was the perfect day. A few fluffy clouds.
Temperatures hovering in the mid-seventies. Relatively
low humidity. It made me want to stay in this moment

forever. My family surrounding me. The best thing that had ever happened to me sitting beside me. All my worries temporarily forgotten.

"Like I said..." I squared my shoulders. "That's bull."

Lachlan's mouth curved up into a playful smile, and I instantly second-guessed myself. "You sure about that? I'll let you retract it this one time."

I pinched my lips together. "You say that *every* time."

"What can I say? I'm a firm believer in giving people a second chance." He winked.

"No need. I stand by my initial determination of your cards being bullshit."

Before Imogene could open her mouth, I slapped a single bill on top of her pile, my eyes not straying from Lachlan's, remaining firm in my resolve.

"You might be disappointed when you flip over my cards, love."

"If this is all part of a ploy so I'll retract my bullshit call, I'm not playing." I grabbed another dollar and handed it to Imogene, my gaze still locked with Lachlan's.

Smirking, he nodded toward the pile of cards. "You can do the honors."

Pulse slowly increasing, I reached for the first card and flipped it over.

"Seven of hearts," Wes announced.

I shot him a glare. "I can see that." I looked back at the pile, ignoring Lachlan's growing smirk when I flipped over the next card.

"Seven of clubs," Eli teased, which earned him a high-five from Lachlan.

"Don't you start, too," I playfully warned my nephew.

Drawing in a deep breath, I reached for the final card, mumbling, "Don't be a seven. Don't be a seven. Don't be a seven."

I flipped it over, the entire table erupting in cheers when the card ended up being a Queen of Hearts.

"Eat it, Hale," I joked, watching in amusement as he organized all the cards in his hand, almost unable to hold them all.

Almost.

The man had enormous hands.

And the things he did with those hands...

"I can still win. I now have an advantage in determining who's bs-ing everyone."

"Okay then." I straightened my spine, placing my last two cards face-down on the table. "Two eights. What say you to that?"

He studied me for a beat, then his hand, then my face again. "Bull is what I say."

I leaned toward him. "Are you sure about that?" I

threw his words back at him. "I'll let you retract it this one time."

He edged closer, his proximity causing a shiver to roll through me.

At first, I was overly cautious about displaying anything remotely resembling affection in front of Imogene and Eli.

Then Wes reminded me it was good for them to see stuff like this. Especially Imogene. That I shouldn't hide my feelings from my daughter. That she needed to see what a healthy relationship looked like so she'd recognize a bad one if, God forbid, she ever found herself in one.

"Flip it, Hale."

He stared at me for a moment, then turned over the two cards.

A chorus of cheers erupted when he revealed I hadn't been lying after all.

Giving him a coy smile, I lifted the imaginary crown off his head. "I'll just take this back. It appears you've been dethroned as the King of Bullshit."

"It appears so." He leaned toward me, pressing a soft kiss to my neck. "But you'll always be my queen, love."

"He's so good with Eli," Londyn commented from Lachlan's chair now that he, Wes, Imogene, and Eli had started up an impromptu game of cornhole. "And Imogene, of course." She gave me an endearing smile. "He's a great guy, Julia." She squeezed my hand. "A really great guy."

"He really is," I replied, turning my gaze back to the yard as Lachlan high-fived Imogene after they sank nearly all their bags in the small opening of the wooden plank several feet away. "I wasn't sure how he was going to handle all of this. Me having a teenage daughter and whatnot." I sighed, shaking my head. "But he's been incredibly patient."

I took a sip of wine, pushing down the feelings of guilt that always seemed to resurface whenever Lachlan joined us for our family gatherings and I saw how great he was with Imogene and Eli.

"What is it?" Londyn narrowed her gaze on me, able to sense my unease.

I hesitated, unsure how to even give voice to what was going through my mind. But if anyone would understand, it was Londyn. After all, she had the unfortunate luck of being one of Nick's early assault victims when she was a student at one of the colleges where he taught.

If she'd never met my brother, if I hadn't seen her strength in saying enough was enough, I doubted I would have found my own strength.

May still have been married to Nick.

Or worse.

A shiver rolled through me at the thought, but I quickly suppressed it.

"When you and Wes first got together," I began, fidgeting with the stem of my wine glass, then lifting my gaze back to hers, "did you ever discuss the future?"

"What do you mean?" She shifted in her chair, attempting to get comfortable around her swollen belly, absentmindedly placing her hand over it. When I glanced at her stomach, realization washed over her face. "Oh."

"Yeah."

"I guess we never really did. After everything I'd been through, I never thought I wanted kids. I'm pretty sure I mentioned something to that effect to Wes, and if memory serves, it didn't faze him. He just wanted to be with me, as he proved through...everything."

A distant expression crossed her dark complexion, but it disappeared just as quickly.

She tilted her head to the side. "Why do you ask?"

"Lachlan and I haven't really discussed it. I know it sounds crazy, since we've only been together a few months. What couple in their right minds has the 'kids talk' this early on in their relationship?" I dropped my voice to a whisper. "But I'm not sure he understands that when I say I can't get pregnant, it's not just because I'm on some sort of birth control."

"And seeing him with Imogene and Eli makes you feel like you're depriving him of something," she said, filling in the blanks.

I shrugged, neither confirming nor denying her statement.

"Listen, Julia..." Londyn placed her hand on mine. "I can't speak for Lachlan about what he wants out of life. Only he can do that. But I see the way he looks at you. The way his eyes light up the second they fall on you."

She leaned toward me the best she could. "Don't let your head get in the way of your happiness. Don't let the games *he* played on you in the past get in the way of your future. You're more than just a womb meant to bear children. If the way I've seen that rather fine specimen of a man treat you is any indication, I'd bet he wouldn't care about that. That, at the end of the day, he just wants to be with you."

I gave her a smile, trying to find some sort of reassurance in her words. But as I turned my attention forward once more, seeing Lachlan joking and laughing with the kids, I couldn't help but think I was depriving him of something he deserved.

A chime from my phone cut through my thoughts, followed by the distant sound of the doorbell echoing from within the house.

I grabbed my cell off the table and opened the door-bell app. When I checked the camera feed, a small ball of apprehension formed in my stomach at the image of Agent Curran standing on my doorstep.

On a Sunday.

"Are you expecting anyone?" Wes shouted as he tossed a bean bag toward the cornhole board. When I didn't immediately respond, he paused, looking my way, Lachlan doing the same.

"It's John Curran."

"The FBI agent?" Londyn asked shakily, eyes wide, breathing increasing.

Wes looked between Imogene and Eli. "You two play by yourselves for a minute." Then he and Lachlan jogged toward us.

"It's nothing you need to concern yourself with," Wes attempted to reassure his wife.

I hated keeping her in the dark. But Wes didn't want to do anything to cause her undue stress, especially this late in her pregnancy. And this most certainly would cause her stress.

A *lot* of stress.

"He's been looking into who could be sending me that jewelry," I told her, doing my best to keep my voice light, as if it weren't a big deal. "I'm sure that's all he's here to discuss. Do you mind keeping an eye on Imogene for a few minutes?"

She looked from me to Wes, then Lachlan, obviously suspicious that we weren't giving her the full story. It wasn't a complete lie, though. Agent Curran *had* been looking into the jewelry. She didn't need to know the jewelry I'd received once belonged to over a dozen women who were now dead.

"Of course," she finally responded, still uneasy.

I gave her an encouraging smile, hiding my own trepidation.

I feared whatever the reason for Agent Curran's visit was about to change everything.

CHAPTER TWENTY-ONE

Julia

"I'm guessing this isn't a social visit," I remarked as I lowered myself onto the couch in my home office, meeting Agent Curran's eyes as he sat in the reading chair opposite me.

Initially, he'd wanted to speak to me in private. While I appreciated the gesture, it wasn't necessary. I didn't keep secrets from my brother. Not anymore. He was as much a part of this as I was.

So was Lachlan.

If a new development affected me, it also affected these two men.

"No, it isn't," Agent Curran replied in his no-

nonsense tone, his expression hard. I doubted I'd ever seen him smile.

Did he even know *how* to smile?

Clearing his throat, he straightened his tie. "As you know, I pulled your ex-husband's visitation log."

I nodded. "Yes. And learned in the weeks leading up to her death, Claire Hale had paid him numerous visits under a media approval."

Agent Curran briefly glanced in Lachlan's direction before returning his gaze to me. "Precisely. Ethan has looked through all of Claire's files for some sort of indication as to what they could have discussed over the course of the roughly twelve hours they spent together."

"But he couldn't find anything."

"Correct. As of now, he's been unsuccessful in finding any of her notes. And given the time constraint we're under, especially now that it's almost October, I thought it might be in our best interests to pursue a second avenue."

"Second avenue?" Wes asked, leaning forward from beside me on the couch, resting his elbows on his knees.

"Yes."

"And what would that be?"

"As an FBI agent, I often check in on offenders I helped put behind bars, especially to ease any victim's concerns."

"And what offender did you check in on?" My voice rose in pitch toward the end.

A hand grasped mine, but I didn't acknowledge it. I couldn't. Not until I heard Agent Curran confirm what I knew in my heart he was about to say.

"Domenic Jaskulski."

I closed my eyes, drawing in a deep breath to settle my nerves. When I reopened them, I gave him a penetrating stare, hoping he wouldn't see my trepidation over the direction I feared this was going.

"Since Ethan couldn't find much information regarding Claire's purpose for her visits, I decided to try my luck and go straight to the source. See if I could get anything out of him."

I barked out a laugh. This was a man who maintained his innocence throughout his trial, even going so far as to fire his attorney and represent himself.

"I doubt he told you anything."

"You're right. But he didn't refuse to help, either."

I straightened, brows furrowing, surprised. "He didn't?"

"No." Agent Curran licked his lips. "He offered to share what he'd discussed with Ms. Hale, but asked for something in return."

"Something in return?" I repeated, a chill washing down my spine.

He nodded slowly.

"And what is this something?" Wes asked, jaw twitching.

"He wants to see you," Agent Curran directed at me.

A stillness washed over the room, no one moving or speaking for several seconds as his answer hung in the air. But it was short-lived. Wes and Lachlan simultaneously jumped up, expressing their mutual abhorrence to the notion.

"Absolutely not!" Lachlan declared, muscles strained, stance wide.

"Out of the question!" Wes added at the same time.

"I don't like it, either," Agent Curran said, attempting to placate both men. He stood, resecuring the button of his suit jacket. "That's why I didn't say anything immediately following my visit with Nick. I'd hoped it wouldn't matter. That Ethan would find something. A missing piece that would answer all our questions.

"Unfortunately, we're no closer to determining who this bastard is than we were when we first figured out the connection between the jewelry you've received and the women they belonged to. These victims have absolutely nothing in common, other than they're dead of what all physical evidence suggests to be suicide. That's the only common thread. In serial cases, there's normally something the victims have in common with each other. Appearance. Age. Socioeconomic background. Profession. Hell, some serial killers target women based on their names. But here... There's nothing."

"Other than the fact each woman had a profession in common with a victim in Nick's case who committed suicide on the same date," Wes snipped out.

"I understand that. But we need something more than a tenuous coincidence. Which is why I think this may be our best course of action right now."

Agent Curran turned his pleading eyes to mine. "Nick knows something that could be useful in finding this bastard. I feel it in my bones. And since Ms. Hale had been looking into this leading up to her death and had visited Nick, I have to think he knows something that could help. I'm fully aware I'm asking a lot of you, especially after everything you endured because of him—"

"All the more reason you shouldn't ask her to do this!" Wes exclaimed, every inch of his body throbbing with fury, eyes wide, muscles tense. It matched Lachlan's reaction. "That bastard abused my sister for years. He may not have left bruises, at least until the end, but the psychological trauma he put her through was just as bad, if not worse. You can't ask her to subject herself to that again."

"I assure you, he will be cuffed, shackled, and chained."

I parted my lips to insert myself into the conversation, considering it was about me, but before I could, Wes continued.

"And will his mouth be duct taped? Because that's the source of most of her trauma."

"I've already spoken with Dr. Fields. She's more than willing to spend some time to prepare Julia, just like she did before Nick's cross-examination of her during his trial. As you know, Dr. Fields has full knowledge of Nick's behavior. She'll give her the tools she needs."

"I—" I began, but Lachlan talked over me.

"A psychologist?" he sneered. "That's your only source of protection when you put her in a room with a complete sociopath? A bloody psychologist?"

"I understand you both care deeply for Julia, and having your support will go a long way here."

"No," Wes declared vehemently. "Under no circumstances is this happening. Not after—"

"*Enough!*" I shot to my feet, unable to stomach hearing these men make decisions for me without even allowing me to voice my own concerns.

Three pairs of eyes darted toward me.

"Will all of you just shut up?!" I fisted my hands, eyes squeezed shut, muscles strained. Inhaling a deep breath, I attempted to calm my irritation as silence hung in the room.

When I opened my eyes again, I focused on Agent Curran. "Where will this meeting take place?"

"Julia...," Lachlan began, advancing. But before he could get too close, I held up a hand, shooting him a warning glare.

He came to an immediate stop, his expression falling.

Then I looked back at Agent Curran, eyebrow raised, awaiting his response.

"I pulled a few strings. Even though this isn't an official investigation, I've managed to secure an interrogation room at the prison. Cameras will be monitoring, and there's a two-way mirror. I'll be in the observation room right next door, as will a handful of guards."

Crossing my arms in front of my chest, I nodded, chewing on my lower lip. Anyone in my position probably wouldn't even consider doing this, not after everything I endured. Not just during our marriage, but for months...years following his arrest.

But I still lived with the guilt of not doing enough. Of not voicing my concerns during my marriage. If I had, some of his victims might still be alive.

What if Nick did hold the answer to what happened to Claire?

What if I could prevent another woman from losing her life in a matter of weeks?

I had to at least try.

"And will anyone else be in the room with me? Besides...*him?*"

Agent Curran slowly shook his head. "I'd hoped to arrange a meeting between glass, but this is his request. A face-to-face meeting. Alone."

"I see."

I stepped toward the bay windows overlooking the back yard, watching as Imogene and Eli kicked a soccer ball around.

"You can't seriously be considering this, Jules," Wes said softly, touching a hand to my shoulder. "Please. Don't you remember everything he did?"

I whirled around, eyes on fire as I leaned toward him. "You think I don't remember all the shit he put me through? I live with the memories every second of my life, Wes. *Every...fucking...second.* And while I appreciate your concern, this isn't your choice." I swung my stare toward Lachlan. "Or yours."

"But—" Wes and Lachlan said at the same time.

"No." I pinned Wes with a glare. "You should know better than anyone precisely why this needs to be my choice. For years, that sick bastard took every single decision away from me. I didn't get to choose what to wear. How to style my hair. What to eat." I threw my hands up in frustration. "Hell, I didn't even get to choose to get pregnant. He stole all that from me."

I swallowed hard past the painful lump forming in

my throat, pushing down the emotions bubbling to the surface.

"So this needs to be my decision. And mine alone."

I glowered at Wes and Lachlan, then returned my attention to Agent Curran.

"When will this take place?"

"At your convenience. We'll need a few days to prepare you. I'm hoping you won't need to spend much time with him. Just enough to satisfy him, then I'll come in and try to get the information. Hopefully seeing you will...soften him up a little, if that makes sense."

I nodded. "Knowing Nick, it makes perfect sense."

After all, it was Nick's weakness for me that caused him to drop his defenses long enough for me to fight back, allowing me to escape when I was confident he was about to kill me.

I turned my gaze back out the windows, a sad smile pulling on my lips as I watched my daughter play with Eli. So carefree. So innocent. So happy.

For years, all I wanted for both Imogene and myself was to finally be able to put the past behind us. To be free from the grip *he* still had on us, even from behind bars.

If agreeing to this had the potential to do just that, I didn't have a choice.

Turning back toward Agent Curran, I nodded. "Okay. I'll do it."

He exhaled a relieved breath, advancing and taking my hand in his, shaking it. "Thank you, Ms. Prescott. You don't know how much I appreciate this."

He held my gaze a moment, then dropped his hold, looking at Wes and Lachlan.

"And I promise both of you, every security protocol will be in place. No harm will come to Julia."

Lachlan leveled a harsh stare on him. "You'd better make bloody sure it doesn't."

CHAPTER TWENTY-TWO

Lachlan

An uneasiness settled over Julia's house the rest of the afternoon and into the evening. She put on a smile in front of Imogene, Eli, and Londyn, but I knew it was forced.

Pretty sure they did, too.

I tried to act as if Agent Curran's visit wasn't a big deal. But I had so many questions. I knew Nick was a horrible person, that he'd manipulated Julia throughout their marriage. But Agent Curran's visit brought into stark focus that there was still so much I didn't know.

So much I couldn't learn even after reading everything I was able find about his case.

"You're doing it again," Julia murmured as we lay in

her bed later that night, my arms wrapped around her, everything peaceful.

Except for my brain.

"Doing what?"

"Thinking. I can hear you."

I opened my mouth, about to tell her it was nothing. That was what the old Lachlan would have done. Avoided having difficult discussions for fear of what they would reveal.

I'd done that with Claire, and now she was dead. I refused to make that mistake again. Especially with Julia.

Touching my hand to her shoulder, I turned her onto her back, then propped myself on my elbow, tracing a circle along her arm.

"What did you mean earlier when you said you didn't decide to become pregnant?"

Her expression fell, a sad smile tugging on her mouth. "Oh."

From the beginning, we'd done everything we could to avoid discussing her past. We didn't have the luxury of doing that anymore. Not with everything going on. It was time to finally face this reality.

And the reality was that her past still tormented her.

She gazed at the ceiling, as if it held the answer she needed.

"I used to have these...episodes."

"Episodes?" I asked, brows furrowed.

She nodded, keeping her eyes trained above. "When I'd lose time."

"Jesus..."

She didn't have to spell it out. I knew enough about Nick to put the pieces together.

"I'd wake up in the morning, unsure what day it was, unable to remember how I even got into bed. When I'd ask Nick what happened, he always told me I had a bit too much to drink, even though I've never been a big drinker. Sure, I enjoy a glass of wine with dinner, but I've never liked being drunk. Or even buzzed. Hate the loss of control. So the idea that I drank to the point of not remembering anything never sat well with me. But there was no other explanation. At least I didn't think there was."

"But you *didn't* drink too much. Did you?" I asked, struggling to keep the anger out of my tone.

"No."

"How often did you...lose time?"

"Not too often at first. Maybe once every few months. But as time went on, it happened more and more frequently."

"And during these episodes..."

"He had sex with me."

"No. He raped you."

"Yes."

"And that's how you got pregnant?"

She nodded. "We'd been married maybe a year at this point. It was before I knew what he was doing. Was actually *how* I learned what he was doing. I hadn't been feeling well. Constantly tired. Nausea. Stuff like that. If we'd been sexually active, I would have taken a pregnancy test. But in the few weeks prior, we hadn't been. At least not to my knowledge. So I went to the doctor."

"And you learned you were pregnant."

"I lost it, Lachlan. When the nurse came in with a smile on her face and congratulated me, I absolutely lost it. I'd always wondered if Nick had something to do with all my lost time." Her chin quivered as tears streamed down her cheeks. "Now I knew."

I pulled her body to mine, kissing her temple, trying to reassure her that I was nothing like him. That I'd never hurt her. That I'd always respect her.

"Did you confront him?"

"Of course. And he did what he did best. Manipulated me into believing I was an overly amorous drunk. That I'd initiated things several times." She pushed out a disbelieving laugh, pulling back to look at me. "Do you want to know the ironic part?"

"What's that?"

"He made it sound like *he* was the one who didn't consent to sex. That *I* forced *him*. Then he casually stated he hadn't told anyone because he didn't want to embarrass me. Didn't want to ruin my reputation. My family's reputation. After all, the Bradfords were prominent in Atlanta society. Something like this could have destroyed them. Could have destroyed Wes."

"So you stayed quiet." My muscles stiffened, anger burning in my veins over the manipulative games that bastard played with her.

"He had me so brainwashed, I thought even if I did say something, nobody would believe me. He was my husband. I was supposed to want to have sex with him. Not cringe in response to his touch. Even back then, even before I knew the truth, it always felt...wrong."

I pinched my lips into a tight line, jaw twitching.

"There was one good thing about being pregnant, though," she muttered.

"What's that?"

"No more lost time," she answered, a sadness in her tone. "He stopped drugging me."

I peered at her, my chest rising and falling in a quicker pattern, nostrils flaring as I attempted to push down the rage...to no avail. I shot up, digging my hands into my hair. I wished I were at my house. Then I could lock myself in the gym for an hour and take out some of this aggression on a punching bag.

Even though I'd really love to use Nick as a punching bag.

Or target practice.

"I want to fucking kill him, Julia," I stated, looking her way, fighting to keep my emotions in check. Something that was growing increasingly more difficult. "He doesn't deserve the air he breathes. He deserves to die the most sadistic death possible. Even then, it won't be enough."

"I did stab him in the balls." She ran a soothing hand down my arm. I should have been the one comforting her, not the other way around. "Well, not directly *in* the balls. Sadly, I missed hitting anything important. Pretty sure he's just shooting blanks now, though."

"But he can still shoot?"

"Yes."

I nodded, taking a moment to process just how depraved this asshole truly was. Then I recalled something Julia had said in Hawaii. Something I'd forgotten. Something I didn't even care about, since I was able to reap the benefits of it.

Now I wondered if there were more to it than I originally thought.

"In Hawaii, you mentioned you couldn't get pregnant..." I lifted my gaze to hers.

I didn't even have to ask. She knew what I was getting at.

"Nick taught at a college in New York for the first year of Imogene's life. She was born with a heart defect that required surgery mere weeks after birth. She's fine now, but because I wanted to keep her near her team of doctors, I stayed in Charleston, where we were living at the time. Since Nick was out of my life for an extended period of time..."

"You were able to have surgery without him knowing."

She nodded. "I had to go through quite a few doctors to find one who would do a tubal ligation for me. It's not as easy as it sounds."

"Why not?"

"I was only twenty-six, in my 'prime child-bearing years', according to a lot of medical practitioners. It didn't matter how vehemently I insisted I didn't want any more children. Many doctors still refused. When I found one who *claimed* to be willing, they wanted to make sure I had my husband's consent." She barked out a laugh. "It didn't matter *I* never consented to him impregnating me in the first place. I needed *his* consent to have a procedure done on my own body."

She drew in a quivering breath, angrily wiping at the tears on her face.

"I was in a really dark place back then. If it weren't for Imogene..." She shook her head. "Well, I doubt I'd be here today if I didn't have her. She saved my life. After watching her little body fight to survive those early days, I knew I needed to fight to survive, too. She became my purpose for living. For everything. She still is."

My heart squeezed at the despair in her words. I was on the verge of restating my argument against her seeing Nick in prison, but she continued before I could, her voice bright, a complete shift from a moment ago.

"Eventually, I found a doctor who would do the procedure, no questions asked. Wes even lent me the money so it wouldn't show up on any insurance statement."

"Did Nick ever find out? Weren't there scars?"

She raised an eyebrow. "Did *you* ever notice scars?"

I shook my head. And I liked to think I knew her body rather intimately.

"They healed pretty quickly. After just a few weeks, it was only a small, red blemish." She pulled the duvet down, revealing her naked torso. Then she pointed to a subtle, pink mark on the right side of her lower abdomen, an identical mark on the opposite side, as well. "It's why I was able to do it. Because I knew the scars would heal quickly. So when I say I can't get pregnant, it's not a case of having some IUD removed. Or even because of my age. I *can't* get pregnant, Lachlan. I made sure it was no longer a possibility years ago."

"Because of Nick," I stated.

She nodded. "Because of Nick."

I closed my eyes as I processed this.

Truthfully, when she'd mentioned she couldn't get pregnant, I assumed it was simply because she was on some form of birth control. Never in my wildest imagination could I have guessed she essentially sterilized herself because of what her asshole ex-husband put her through.

He deserved getting stabbed in the balls.

Hell, he deserved worse than that. Deserved to spend years living in fear for his life, like Julia still did.

"If that's a dealbreaker, I understand," Julia interjected when I didn't immediately say anything. "You're young. You have your entire life ahead of you. I can't give you a family. I saw you with Nikko. Know how close you were with Claire. With your mother. You'll never have that with me. And every time I watch you with Eli or Imogene, or remember how amazing you were with all those kids in your Little League, all I can think is that now I'm the one who's going to steal something from you. Like Nick stole so much from me."

I cupped her face in my hands, my gaze unwavering as I peered into her eyes, not allowing her to look away.

"Don't. Don't even think like that, Julia. I don't care about any of that."

"But you *should* care, Lachlan. You should really consider if I'm worth giving all that up. Because that's exactly what you'd have to do to be with me. Give up any dreams of having your own children."

"That's not a dealbreaker for me. I haven't thought

about having children of my own in years. Not since..." I trailed off, not needing to say it. Julia understood.

I swiped away a few of her tears with my thumbs. "If being with you has taught me anything, it's that sometimes dreams change. *You're* my dream now. What's it going to take for you to realize that? To realize you deserve to be happy? That *you* make me happier than I thought possible. Like I said in Hawaii..." I curved toward her. "I just want to be with you. Nothing more. Nothing less." My lips brushed hers.

"Nothing less," she repeated against my mouth.

I rested my forehead on hers, closing my eyes as I savored in this connection. Prayed it would be strong enough to help us weather the storm I sensed brewing offshore.

"Nothing less."

CHAPTER TWENTY-THREE

Julia

An arm crept across my torso, stirring me from a fitful night's sleep. Every time I closed my eyes, all I could see was Nick's threatening glare.

Was I really strong enough to be in the same room as him?

It was bad enough he ended up representing himself during the trial. As such, he had the right to cross-examine me, as well as every other victim who'd agreed to testify against him, albeit with standby counsel present to intervene in the event Nick grew verbally abusive.

I'd hoped that would be the last time I'd ever have to face him.

Now I was about to willingly sit in the same room. Alone.

I just had to remind myself that I wasn't the same woman I was all those years ago. I was so much stronger now. I'd built a life without him. Built a family without him. Survived without him.

I had to believe I'd survive this, too.

When Lachlan caressed the scar by my right hip, his motions gentle and affectionate, I moaned, melting into his warmth. He brushed my hair over my shoulder, peppering kisses along my nape, his touch becoming increasingly sensual.

He rocked his hips against me, his erection prominent. As his hand slid past my torso and toward my thighs, I parted them. His thumb landed on my clit, and relief washed over me. This was exactly what I needed.

Needed to return to this place with Lachlan where the only thing that mattered was him, me, and the incredible pleasure we shared on a daily basis.

"Say you want me," he growled, his breathing growing labored.

"I want you."

"Say you need me."

"I need you."

"And I need you." He brought his erection up and slowly eased inside me. It didn't matter how many times we'd done this very thing. That first thrust always stole my breath. "So fucking much."

I parted my lips, savoring in his warmth as he filled me before retreating, continuing the same, erotic rhythm. With each push and retreat, he became more desperate. More frenzied. More impassioned.

"Say you're mine." When he drove into me this time, it was borderline painful.

I released a cry. Something about this was off. As if he were staking his claim.

"I'm yours," I whimpered.

"Mine."

He bit my neck. But it wasn't the soft nibble that was Lachlan's norm. It caused a shot of anguish to course through me.

"Lachlan..."

I squirmed, growing increasingly uncomfortable as he picked up his pace, his teeth clamping onto my skin to the point I was convinced he drew blood.

"You're mine. Forever." With each word, his thrusts became more painful. Excruciating. Harrowing.

"Stop," I begged, attempting to free myself from his touch.

But he didn't. In fact, my pleas only seemed to encourage him to fuck me harder.

More brutally.

"Never. I'll never stop. Never stop taking what's mine."

His voice came out strained. It didn't sound like Lachlan. I couldn't even make out the accent that made my toes curl. His tone was different. Ominous. Threatening.

I bucked against him, trying to get him off me. He responded by holding me tighter, locking me in place. Then he pulled out of me, making me exhale in relief.

But it was short-lived.

A hand on my shoulder, he pressed me onto my back, his body smothering mine.

My gaze finally met his.

Instead of a pair of vibrant, blue eyes staring back, they were a threatening dark brown.

Adrenaline rushed through me as I fought against the body restraining me. What the hell was going on? Nothing about this made any sense. All I knew was the man on top of me wasn't Lachlan.

Instead, he looked far too much like my ex-husband.

"No use fighting me. You'll never win. Like I promised..."

He brought his hand to my neck, wrapping his fingers around it and squeezing. But unlike when Lachlan did this same thing, his touch sensual and erotic, this was more possessive.

More deadly.

"Till death do us part, Julia."

He tightened his hold, cutting off my oxygen. I writhed beneath him, clawing at his hand and arm. But he used his own imposing body to keep me bound to the bed, unable to escape. To run. To ever be free.

"Till death do us part."

I fought against him, using every ounce of strength I possessed to free myself — scratching, kicking, flailing... to no avail.

I was about to give up when I heard a familiar voice call my name.

I tried to respond, but no sound came, the hand around my throat making it impossible.

"Julia!" the voiced shouted again, terrified and desperate.

Abruptly, the weight crushing me was gone, my airway clear.

Flinging my eyes open, I shot up in bed, gasping. I was instantly met with a pair of blue eyes, Lachlan staring at me in concern, fear oozing from every one of his pores.

I blinked, panting, taking in my surroundings. I was in my bed. In my room. In my house.

Where Nick was moments ago.

I was certain of it.

"Imogene... Is she okay?" I scrambled out of the sweaty sheets and stood, my legs nearly giving out beneath me. I grabbed onto the headboard to steady myself, fighting against the dizzy spell enveloping me, my body shaking.

"Hey." Lachlan clambered out of the bed, rushing to my side. He looped his arm around my waist, spinning me to face him. "What's going on?"

"He was here. What if—"

"Who was here?"

"Nick. Didn't you see him?"

Lachlan stared at me, a mixture of worry and something resembling pity crossing his features. "It was a dream, Julia. Or, more appropriately, a nightmare. You were screaming and thrashing in your sleep. I kept trying to wake you up."

He bit his lower lip, eyes glossy. Then he pulled me in tightly, not caring my body was drenched with sweat, and buried his head in my neck.

"You scared me, love."

I drew in a shuddering breath, working to shake off the disquieting episode, my body still trembling. It all felt so real.

Normally when I dreamed, everything was detached. Like I was a bystander watching the events unfold. But I knew it wasn't real. Knew I'd soon wake up and forget everything my brain conjured.

Not this time.

I still felt Nick's hand on my throat, breath scalding my skin, body covering mine.

"It's okay," I finally said, shaking it off. "I'm okay. Like you said..." I pulled back, giving Lachlan a reassuring smile, not wanting him to read too much into this. "It was just a dream. Nothing to be worried about."

I stepped out of his hold, avoiding his gaze as I padded across the room and into the bathroom, closing the door.

Peering into the mirror, I studied my appearance, almost expecting to see teeth marks and bruising on my neck.

Nothing.

I blew out a shaky breath. It truly was just a dream. Simply my overactive imagination at work. My greatest fears realized.

Turning on the faucet, I cupped the cold water in my trembling hands and splashed it on my face. When I straightened and returned my gaze to the mirror, I jumped and let out a small gasp at the figure behind me, my heart ricocheting into my throat until my eyes had a chance to focus.

Lachlan studied me intently. "It's *not* nothing," he said gruffly, handing me a towel.

I took it from him, dabbing the water from my face.

"Your reaction just now confirmed it." He paused, licking his lips. "It was about *him*, wasn't it?"

I didn't respond.

He crossed his arms in front of his chest, biceps straining, jaw twitching. Several silent moments passed as we simply stared at each other. I could practically hear the battle being waged in his head.

"I don't want you to do this," he said, voice determined, yet with a touch of vulnerability.

I was about to reiterate the same argument I made yesterday, but before I could, he held up his hand.

"I know. You want this to be your choice. And I appreciate your reasoning. But is it *really* your choice?"

I looked at him quizzically, brows furrowed. "What do you mean?"

"How can it be *your* choice when this is exactly what *he* wants? For you to play into his hand? You may think you're the one making the decision here, but this is just another case of him manipulating you. Exerting his power over you. Controlling you."

"He doesn't control me," I argued back, placing my hands on my hips.

Lachlan barked out a laugh, biting and harsh. "Sure he doesn't."

"What's that supposed to mean?"

"Do you listen to yourself, Julia?" He edged toward me. "That bastard still has his claws in you. And you fucking let him."

"I do not."

"Okay." He stepped back, widening his stance. "Come to California with me this week. Let me introduce you to some of my good mates on the team. Let me take you to dinner. Let me show you off. Kiss you in public. Act like I'm actually your bloody boyfriend instead of just some dirty little secret you let fuck you when you need to get off."

"That's not all you are to me, and you know it. I've told you time and time again how much you mean to me."

"But when are you going to *show* me?" He drew in a deep breath, softening his voice. "Please, Julia. Be with me. And not just behind closed doors, but out in the open, too."

I lifted my eyes to his, hope and desperation swirling in his brilliant, blue orbs. Parting my lips, I paused, then shook my head. "I can't."

His shoulders fell, expression pinching. "Can't? Or won't?"

"That's not it. Imogene—"

"Of course." He threw his hands up. "Imogene... Are you always going to use her as an excuse?"

"She's not an excuse. She—"

"Yes, she is!" he roared, advancing. Out of instinct, I backed up, flattening my spine against the wall.

Regret instantly covered his features. He halted,

sucking in a calming breath before focusing his attention back on me.

"You use her as an excuse for bloody everything, Julia," he continued, calmer. "You have from the beginning. And I fucking get it, okay? This is scary for you. It's scary for me, too. I'm trying here, Julia. So bloody hard. But I feel like no matter what I do, no matter how much I love you, it'll never be enough."

I inhaled sharply, darting my wide eyes to his, a mixture of excitement and dread filling me as his confession hung in the air.

"What did you say?" I whispered.

He stepped toward me, framing my face in his hands. "I love you," he confessed, not shying away from it.

Not like I so often did when discussing my emotions. After a lifetime of constantly having someone use my feelings against me, it was a pre-programmed response.

"Maybe you think it's too soon, since we've only known each other a few months. But if losing Piper and my sister taught me anything, it's that we should tell people how we feel about them every chance we get. So that's what I'm doing. Not holding back. Not letting fear control me. Because make no mistake about it, Julia..."

His hold on my face tightened, eyes searing me.

"This fucking petrifies me. But I love you. And I'm not telling you this so you'll say it back. I get that you have a lot more to work through than I do." He licked his lips. "I'm telling you this because you deserve to know that you're loved. That you don't have to live in fear anymore." He inched toward me. "That you don't have to let him control you anymore.

"Please... Don't let him do this. Don't go see him."

"If he knows something—"

"I understand why you feel like you have to do this," he interrupted. "You feel guilty that you didn't do enough to prevent harm from coming to all those women. If anyone appreciates that kind of guilt, it's me. I killed my girlfriend. Me. And not because of some indirect cause or failure to act. I picked up a gun, knowing I could barely see more than an inch in front of me, and fired."

"Yes, but you were trying to protect her. I—"

"For the longest time, I wore that guilt like a goddamn badge of honor. Convinced myself I didn't deserve to be happy. I put up wall after wall, refusing to allow people in. But *you* made me realize I *do* deserve to be happy." He paused. "When are you going to realize you deserve to be happy, too? When are you going to finally let me in?"

I shook my head, chest aching. "I don't think I know how."

He closed his eyes, disappointment covering every

inch of him as he dropped his hold on me and stepped back, increasing the distance between us.

"Maybe you need to figure that out," he choked out on a quiver. "Because if this is all you're going to give me, if you're always going to keep me at arm's length, it doesn't matter how much I love you. It will never be enough."

A chill consumed me, my throat constricting. "What are you saying?"

"I'm saying you need to make a decision, Julia. You can either be with me completely...or not be with me at all. I can't live in the middle anymore. Can't be in a relationship with someone who perpetually has one foot out the door. So until you're ready to jump into this with both feet, I can't continue giving you my heart only for you to keep destroying it. Because that's what this is doing, Julia. It's fucking destroying me. And I know it's destroying you, too. You're just too damn stubborn to admit it. "

"Lachlan, I—"

"I'm begging you. Be with me. Choose me. Not him. Don't go see him. Don't give him the satisfaction."

I swallowed hard at the emotion radiating off him, coupled with his passionate plea.

It should have been so easy to tell him I chose him. That I'd ignore Nick's request.

But I couldn't. Not with everything at stake.

Maybe Lachlan was right and this was another instance of Nick manipulating me. But I had to try.

I'd lived the past several years with the regret of not doing enough.

I couldn't have this on my conscience, too.

Even if it meant losing the best thing that had ever happened to me.

Lachlan should have understood why I had to do this. If he couldn't support my decision, couldn't *respect* my decision, maybe he wasn't the man I thought he was.

"I have to do this."

He squeezed his eyes shut, every inch of his body so tense I feared he was about to shatter into tiny pieces.

Then he stormed out of my room, slamming the door behind him.

CHAPTER TWENTY-FOUR

Lachlan

I collapsed onto my couch, running my hands over my face.

Was I too harsh?

Did I take out my frustrations with Nick on Julia?

From the beginning, I swore I'd be patient with her. But, my god, did she not see what he was doing to her? Was she really that blind?

Or did she not care? Did she see it, yet still allowed it anyway?

I didn't know what it was like to live with a manipulative asshole. Maybe I'd permitted my anger to control me instead of responding rationally.

But my heart physically ached over the idea of that

bastard always coming between us. And that was precisely what was happening now. He was coming between us.

Glancing at my watch, I exhaled deeply. My driver would be here to take me to the airport soon, and I hadn't even begun to think about packing. As much as I hated leaving for over a week with everything in a state of flux, maybe time away was exactly what I needed.

Exactly what Julia needed, too.

I pulled myself off the couch and padded toward the staircase, pausing when the doorbell rang. I furrowed my brows, checking my watch to make sure I hadn't misread it.

I hadn't.

"Maybe he's early," I mumbled, retreating into the foyer and opening the door.

I parted my lips to tell the man I needed ten minutes, then stopped when I saw it wasn't my driver

Instead, it was Detective Walker, his pompous demeanor masked with a congenial smile.

This was the first time I'd seen him since I sent him to the hospital. But just as my agent had informed me, it seemed any damage I did was minor. Then again, it *had* been nearly three months.

His busted lip had healed, his jaw not showing any signs of trauma. Other than his nose appearing a bit more crooked than it did before, he looked like the same prick he was when he refused to investigate my sister's death.

"Detective Walker."

"Mr. Hale. So glad I caught you before you left town. You've got some road games coming up, don't you?"

I nodded. "Which I need to pack for. So, if you don't mind—"

"I'll make this brief. May I come in?"

I crossed my arms in front of my chest, widening my stance. "What's this regarding?"

"Any reason you're being defensive?"

"I don't let people who show up unexpectedly into my house. Especially cops. I don't exactly get a warm, fuzzy feeling from you, Detective."

"I did try calling before simply showing up. As did Detective Marshall with Honolulu PD."

I blinked, my expression momentarily falling.

A detective with HPD *had* reached out to me to go over the statement I'd made after Piper's death. Between baseball and spending every free minute I had with Julia, it had slipped my mind. Didn't think it was important since I gave my statement all those years ago and nothing had changed.

"According to her, she's been trying to reach you for over a month now," Detective Walker continued.

"I've been busy. The playoffs are coming up."

"I understand. But after she couldn't get in touch with you, she asked if I could help. See if I'd have better luck. So I'm here on behalf of the Honolulu Police Department to ask you a few questions about the statement you gave regarding the home invasion you were involved in five years ago. As you know, they've reopened the investigation."

"Nothing in my original statement has changed."

"Then this should take no time at all." He raised an expectant brow, waiting for me to invite him inside.

I hesitated, part of me wanting to tell him any questions he had could be asked right here. But the last thing I wanted was for some reporter to drive by and see me talking to a detective. I could only imagine the rumors that would cause, especially considering it was the same detective I had issues with just a few months ago.

"Fine." I stepped back, allowing him to enter my house, but stopped in the foyer, not inviting him any farther.

"Is there somewhere we can sit?" he asked.

"We can stand. Like you said. This won't take long."

He glared at me for several moments, hoping I'd cave. But I wouldn't. Not today. And not to him.

"As you wish," he eventually relented with a sigh, withdrawing a small notepad from the inside pocket of his suit jacket. "I hoped you could walk me through the events leading up to the home invasion."

"I made a statement during the initial investigation. Nothing has changed. Everything Detective Marshall needs is there."

"Funny you should mention that." With a conniving smile, he flipped through his notepad. "According to Detective Marshall, she uncovered another witness. Someone who'd seen Piper that afternoon. Do you know an Aaliyah Downs?"

An uneasiness settled in my stomach, but I shrugged it off. "She was one of Piper's best friends."

"Piper met her for a coffee that afternoon. Correct?"

"If you're wondering why that wasn't in my statement, it's because I didn't know she'd met up with Aaliyah. She told me she was running to the store to pick up a few things."

"Of course. Of course," Detective Walker said with what felt like feigned sympathy. "That's not what I'm getting at. I'm wondering if you were aware of what they discussed that afternoon."

"Sorry, but the next time I saw Piper, she was being brutally raped. I didn't think to ask if anything else had happened while she was out," I shot back sarcastically. "Like I said, I didn't even know Piper had met up with Aaliyah until the police conducted their investigation."

"Their investigation..." Detective Walker laughed under his breath.

I straightened, eyes narrowing. "What's that supposed to mean?"

"Detective Marshall's a seasoned investigator. When I was just a lowly sergeant, she was my mentor here in Atlanta before wanting a change of scenery. Did you know that?"

I kept my expression even, unsure if it were a good thing this woman was once Detective Walker's superior. If she were anything like him, I had a feeling I wouldn't like her, either.

"Do you want to know what she found interesting?"

"What's that?"

"That the lead detective who worked the initial investigation didn't think to ask what Aaliyah and Piper had talked about. All he did ask was whether she acted out of character. If Aaliyah had seen anyone following her, especially someone matching Caleb Binnick's description." He plastered a fabricated smile onto his face. "You see, that's what we like to call a leading question. Not all that reliable, since it tends to take away a witness' ability to think for him or herself."

"I'm not sure what that has to do with my statement."

"Actually, a fair bit. When Detective Marshall paid Ms. Downs a visit a few weeks ago, she *did* ask what they talked about. And do you want to know what that was?"

"What's that?" I asked softly, my uneasiness growing with every passing moment.

"It was quite interesting. Ms. Downs mentioned that you and Piper had gotten into an argument, and that's why she left the house. Not because she needed to go to the store."

"She *did* say she needed to go to the store," I argued in my defense.

He arched a brow. "Are you admitting you did get into an argument?"

I remained silent for several seconds, glaring at him, jaw clenched. Then I nodded curtly.

"About?"

I sighed, shaking my head. The last thing I wanted to do was tell this clown about it, considering I never mentioned it to anyone. I didn't see how it had anything to do with finding out who assaulted Piper. I was already weighed down with enough remorse over the events that transpired that night. Telling everyone the last words we spoke to each other were in anger would only burden me even more.

"I'd just been promoted to the majors. Along with that came a huge increase in pay. The first thing I did was sign a lease on a great apartment near Downtown Atlanta. The next was buy her a ring."

"How did that go?" There was a smugness in his tone.

"It didn't."

"So you never proposed?"

I pushed out a long breath, running my fingers through my hair, getting more and more agitated. "I guess I did. It certainly didn't go like I'd planned."

"How so?"

"I told her about my promotion, which she didn't seem enthusiastic about. Not like you'd expect when telling your girlfriend of over five years that you'd achieved everything you've ever dreamed of. Then I told her we'd never have to worry about money again. That we wouldn't have to do the long-distance thing, either. That we could live in Atlanta during baseball season, then in Hawaii during the off-season."

"I take it she didn't like that plan."

"She was a competitive surfer. Atlanta isn't exactly near the ocean. So she accused me of not caring about her dreams. But I *did* care. I just hated living so far apart from her. So I proposed. Not sure what I thought it would fix. I was only twenty-two, so I guess you could say I was young and impulsive."

"And how did she respond?"

I shoved my hands into my pockets. "Said she needed to get some air. Think about some things. That she was going to run to the store and we'd discuss everything once I'd had a nap."

"And after she left?"

I swallowed hard. "The next time I saw her, some bastard was holding her down on the bed in the rental unit of my property."

He nodded, seemingly unmoved by the image I'd painted. After making a few notes in his pad, he met my eyes once more.

"Help me understand something. And I hope I'm not stepping on Detective Marshall's toes here, but since she couldn't reach you, you're left to deal with me. At least for the time being. Why didn't you mention anything about this argument during the initial investigation?"

"I don't know." I shook my head. "Maybe because I knew how it would look. The second I'd mention I got into an argument with my girlfriend, then shot her by accident when I was trying to take out her attacker, people would question the validity of my statement."

"And how do you think it looks now that it's five years later and we're just learning you grossly misrepresented your statement?"

"I didn't misrepresent. I just didn't think it necessary to include something that had absolutely nothing to do with what happened to Piper."

"Oh, but that's where you're wrong, Mr. Hale. Because that information *was* necessary." His expression hardened, the vein in his forehead becoming more pronounced.

"How? That argument was completely unrelated to the fact that some prick broke into our house. Gave me a concussion and shattered my knee. Stabbed my sister in the stomach. Then assaulted Piper."

"Speaking of which... Can you tell me why you can't remember what your assailant looked like?" He glanced back down at his notepad. "According to your statement, when you heard someone in the rental unit of your duplex, where you'd been napping, you went into the kitchen."

I puffed out my chest, holding my head high. I easily had about four inches on this guy, but with the direction his line of questioning was taking, I couldn't help but feel small compared to him.

"That's true."

"Yet you can't remember anything about his appearance?" He peered at me with increasing suspicion. I was on the verge of asking if I should call my lawyer. But I did nothing wrong.

"I was jet-lagged." My words were harsh and biting. "And it was dark. I only had a second to realize what was going on before he came after me with one of my own goddamn bats."

"But you regained consciousness after about ten minutes, correct? Your statement indicates you crawled into the bedroom where he was forcing himself on Piper."

"That's correct."

"And you still can't pick out some sort of identifying characteristic, other than medium height and build?"

"Being as thorough as you are," I snipped out sarcastically, "I'm sure you've reviewed my medical file. I had a severe concussion. It was a miracle I even survived. Everything was... Everything was blurry. I thought I was about to lose my vision altogether."

He nodded, jotting down a few more notes. Then he closed his pad, shoving it into his pocket.

"Well, that's all Detective Marshall wanted me to clear up with you. I'll be sure to pass this information along to her. Thanks for your time."

I barely acknowledged him as he turned, making his way to my front door. He was about to open it when he paused, facing me once more.

"Can I ask one more question? For my own...edification."

"What's that?"

"You're left-handed, correct?"

"Yes...," I drew out.

"Interesting."

I widened my stance once more. "Why is that interesting?"

The corners of his mouth curved up. "According to the medical reports, forensics concluded that, based on the shape and direction of Claire's stab wound, it was most definitely inflicted by someone who was left-handed."

I glowered at him, fury scalding my veins. My nostrils flared, jaw ticking, every muscle in my body vibrating with a hatred I didn't think possible. I clenched and unclenched my fists, struggling to reel in the anger dying to be unleashed on him for a second time.

"Get the fuck out of my house," I growled, the deep rumble of my voice echoing against the cathedral ceilings in my foyer, "before I break your jaw, you fucking bastard."

He didn't appear the least bit intimidated, his smug smile only growing.

"I'd be careful if I were you. Threatening law enforcement won't look too good for you. Especially after your recent...difficulty."

"Get. Out."

He opened the door, stepping onto my front porch. Then he glanced over his shoulder. "I wouldn't plan any trips out of the country in the near future."

"Is that a threat?"

"Not at all. Consider it a...friendly piece of advice."

"Well, here's a friendly piece of advice for you, Detective. Go fuck yourself." I slammed the door in his face.

CHAPTER TWENTY-FIVE

Julia

My stomach churned as I stood in a stark, brightly lit observation room in the prison. I couldn't believe I was actually going to do this. That I was mere moments away from being face-to-face with Nick. There were so many times in the past hour I'd considered backing out, especially as Agent Curran led me through the process of entering the prison, which was enough to make anyone have second thoughts, even if visiting a loved one.

But I wasn't visiting a loved one.

I was here to see the man who'd destroyed my life.

All reason told me I should walk away. That

Lachlan was right. That by agreeing to do this, I'd become nothing more than a pawn to Nick yet again.

I'd essentially lost Lachlan over this decision. So I couldn't back out now. Then it would have been for nothing.

An obnoxious buzzing caused me to snap out of my thoughts. I tore my gaze to the two-way mirror, the seconds seeming to stretch as I watched the door open, two guards leading a man into the interrogation room.

A man with whom I once shared a life.

A man who manipulated me at every turn.

A man I'd hoped to never see again.

A sudden wave of nausea overtook me, my knees wobbling.

"Hey," Wes said, catching me as I wavered. "You don't have to do this. You can still back out."

"No, I can't. I have to do this."

"It really could be just a ploy." He narrowed his gaze on me, his voice barely audible as he reiterated Lachlan's argument. Something he'd agreed with when I told him about our fight.

And breakup.

"I'm fine. I'll be fine. He can't hurt me anymore. I won't let him."

I drew in a steadying breath, returning my eyes to the glass. My hands trembled when I saw Nick staring directly at me, as if able to sense exactly where I stood.

It was the first time I'd seen him since the judge sentenced him to serve several life sentences for the crimes he'd committed.

He'd certainly aged the past several years, his blond hair much lighter, face sporting a few more wrinkles, especially around his eyes and lips. But he still had a handsome, distinguished appearance.

Too bad his soul was as ugly as they came.

"Just remember what Dr. Fields told you," Agent Curran encouraged, approaching. "Stay aloof and completely disinterested. Do your best to not show any emotion. If at any time it's too much, just get up and walk toward the door. We'll know you're done at that point."

I nodded, blowing out a breath, taking a moment to settle my nerves.

I could do this. I *had* to do this. Had to show Nick I wasn't the easily controlled and manipulated woman he knew all those years ago. Maybe this was what I'd needed to do all along in order to finally close this chapter of my life.

"Okay. I'm ready."

"Okay."

Wes gave me one last hug, squeezing me tightly. Then I followed Agent Curran toward the door. Just as he was about to open it, a guard entered...

So did Lachlan.

I stiffened, surprised. Not only because he was supposed to be out of town, but also because of how we left things earlier in the week. I hadn't even told him I'd be seeing Nick today. Didn't think it mattered.

I thought we were done.

Maybe we weren't.

"What are you doing here?"

"Wes told me you were coming here today."

"But you're supposed to be in California."

He smiled shyly, running his fingers through his hair. "I thought it more important I be here. Show my support."

I stared at him for several seconds, shaking my head.

After our argument, Lachlan was the last person I expected to see. But the fact he was here, that he somehow managed to swallow his pride and do what he felt I needed, meant the world to me.

Walking toward him, I wrapped my arms around him, sighing at how perfect his body felt against mine. He hesitated, then pulled me into his embrace. I inhaled his scent, drawing comfort and strength from the familiarity.

"I've missed this," I confessed, ignoring the fact that we had an audience. That was the least of my worries right now. All I did care about was savoring in the warmth of Lachlan's arms around me.

"I've missed this, too."

Cupping my face in his hands, he rested his forehead on mine. As he pushed out a tiny puff of air, I did the same, exchanging my breath with his, the connection I'd felt from that first night strengthening with every second.

"Be fearless," he said, pulling back and gazing into my eyes. "Show him he doesn't scare you anymore. That he can't get to you anymore. That he has no power over you anymore."

"I will."

"Good." He leaned down, brushing a soft kiss against my temple before stepping away.

"Ready?" Agent Curran asked with a raised brow.

I took one last deep breath, then nodded. "Ready."

He opened the door, and I followed, pausing to glance over my shoulder one last time, giving Lachlan a small smile. Then I joined Agent Curran in the hallway, walking to the interrogation room door.

"Remember what I said..." He faced me. "If at any time you no longer feel comfortable, get up and walk to the door. I'll take over from there. He won't be able to follow you. Won't be able to touch you. He'll be chained to the table. He can't hurt you. Okay?"

"Okay."

"Okay," he repeated, then nodded at the guard.

After swiping his keycard, the guard pressed his thumb against the scanner. The door buzzed, followed by a click. Agent Curran grabbed the handle and, giving me one last encouraging look, opened the door.

The instant I crossed the threshold, Nick swung his gaze to mine, his eyes still as cold and threatening as they were during our marriage.

"My beautiful Julia..."

The sound of his voice made bile rise in my throat. My knees nearly buckled, but I quickly recovered, squaring my shoulders, not wanting to give him the pleasure of seeing so much as a hint of weakness.

He attempted to get up, momentarily forgetting about the shackles keeping him bound to the metal table.

"Please excuse my lack of manners," he said in a low, Southern drawl. "Unfortunately, it's out of my control at the moment."

I cautiously made my way to the chair on the opposite side of the table, doing my best to keep as much space between us as possible. Nick's gaze didn't stray from me, the way he stared at me making my skin crawl.

Which was probably exactly what he wanted.

"My god...," he exhaled once I finally sat down, a twisted look of awe on his face. "You are just as beautiful as you were on our wedding day. My heart..." He attempted to cover his chest with his hand, the restraints stopping him. "It still skips a beat at your mere presence. Tell me, my love..." He leaned toward me, a dangerous glint in his eyes. "Do I still have that effect on you? Pulse racing, stomach fluttering, all-consuming need? I'll be honest..."

He swept his gaze over my body. The way he looked at me made me queasy, but I swallowed down any trepidation, feigning indifference.

"I thought you were stunning as a blonde, but this shade of red is quite becoming on you. Then again, I'll always consider you the most beautiful woman to ever walk the earth. My eternal beloved. My Hera." He dropped his voice, something sinister creeping into his tone. "My wife."

"I am *not* your wife," I reminded him harshly.

"Maybe not according to the State of Georgia, but in my heart, you will always belong to me. Just as I will always belong to you. We are forever connected. Nothing you do will change that."

I considered arguing against his assertion, but it wasn't worth it. He *wanted* me to argue. I wasn't going to give him the satisfaction. Wasn't going to play into his hand.

"Speaking of which, how's my daughter?"

"She's not your daughter. Not anymore."

"Again..." His jaw tensed, my answer clearly getting under his skin. "The same argument I made for that ridiculous petition for divorce stands for you terminating my parental rights. I will always be a part of Imogene. You will always see me when you look at her." He curved even closer. "She's always had my eyes and smile. Does she still?"

"Imogene's her own person. You have no influence over her."

"And how about you? Do I still have the same hold over you?"

Refusing to answer for fear of what he'd see, I stood, crossing my arms in front of my chest. "I came to see you, as you requested. Now you can answer Agent Curran's questions. Enjoy prison, Nick." I started toward the door.

"I don't think so, Julia. We're not done yet."

I faced him again, more annoyed than anything. "You promised. You said if I came to visit you, you'd tell Agent Curran what you discussed with Claire Hale."

"I said no such thing. Not once did I state or imply that I would tell *him* about my conversations with Ms. Hale." His lips curved into a smirk.

I knew this look. I'd seen it whenever he was about to unleash one of his stupid mind games on me.

"After all, Zeus only answers to one person."

"Hera," I exhaled, momentarily lightheaded.

"I'll happily discuss my rather illuminating conversations with Ms. Hale. But not with Agent Curran. With you. And only you."

I hesitated, glancing between the door and Nick. I had the power to end this. Didn't have to stay here. This wasn't part of the deal. I was supposed to visit Nick as a token of good faith, then be free to walk away. Sitting in the same room and trying to question him when I had no experience in anything like this never factored into it.

It was another one of his games.

One I knew I shouldn't play.

But I'd already come this far. I couldn't walk away without anything to show for it.

"Fine." I spun around, striding back to the table and plopping down onto the chair, leaning back into it. "Tell me what you know. But you do understand how ridiculous this is, considering you're fully aware he's watching this entire thing."

Nick grinned, briefly shifting his gaze past me and to the two-way glass. "Of course I do." He refocused his attention on me. "But as *you* should have figured out by now, I don't give anything away freely. There's always a cost."

"What do you want, Nick?"

"Oh, Julia... There are so many ways I could answer that, but if I told you what I *really* want, I fear the fine, upstanding gentlemen who work for the Department of Corrections would pull me out of here in a heartbeat. Send me back for diagnostic testing to see if perhaps I should be reclassified to the Special Management Unit instead of in this maximum-security hell. So, instead, I'll settle for...a game."

I straightened. "A game?"

"I must confess, life in prison has been trying, my darling. I've been forced to converse with the bottom rung of society, most of whom barely have anything more than a high school education. And that's just the guards. My fellow inmates..." He shivered dramatically. "Suffice it to say, I do miss being able to speak with someone who possesses a higher level of education. Or at least someone who can hold their own in a lively discussion. You've always had a spark, Julia. Always had a gift for engaging people in conversation. Even when we were kids together in that dreadful foster home, I was drawn to you."

"What kind of game are you proposing?" I shifted in the chair, unsure which made me more uncomfortable — the hard metal or Nick's penetrating stare.

"Tit for tat, my love. You answer one of my questions, and I'll tell you one thing I discussed with Ms. Hale. Full disclosure, though. She visited me quite often prior to her tragic death." His eyes gleamed. "This could go on for hours. Days. But I assure you..." He looked up, staring at the two-way glass, "and Agent Curran..." He returned his gaze to mine, "by the end, I'll have shared everything we discussed. But only with you."

He paused, allowing his offer to have a moment to marinate.

"So, what say you? Shall we have a game, Julia?"

I licked my lips, my gaze shifting between the door and Nick. This was quickly becoming more than I bargained for. More than any of us bargained for.

But it was too late to stop this runaway train now. All I could do was follow it all the way to the scene of the crash.

"Let's play."

A slow smile pulled on his lips, his eyes alight with a disturbing kind of excitement.

"Marvelous."

CHAPTER TWENTY-SIX

Julia

"Did Claire want to discuss the recent suicides?" I asked, not wasting a second.

As expected, Nick had other plans.

"Not so fast, my love." He tsked. "Did you forget the parameters I just set forth? I get to ask a question first. After you answer, and only then, will I answer one in return."

I glowered at him for several moments, then squared my shoulders, acting as unaffected as possible. "Fine. What do you want to know?"

"Have you been faithful to me, like I have to you?"

I barked out a laugh that echoed against the walls of

the sterile room. "Faithful? Are you delusional? You weren't even faithful to me during our marriage, Nick."

"My body may not have been, but my heart has always belonged to you. That's what counts. That my heart has always remained true. Even in this...purgatory I seem to have landed in." He looked around the room before leveling his stare back on me. "Now answer me. Have you remained faithful? Or have you been with someone else?"

"I have no reason to be faithful to you, Nick," I responded flippantly, not looking directly at him. "We're not married anymore. I'm free to be with whomever I want."

He set his hands on the table, the chains of his handcuffs scraping against the surface. "That's not an answer, Julia. Have you been with another man since me?" His tone was calm. Even.

It always was.

"For your information, I have been with another man since you. A man whose dick still works. And quite well, if I do say so myself."

His pompous expression momentarily faltered, upper lip quivering.

"My turn," I said when he didn't immediately offer a response, his demeanor still mildly agitated. "Did Claire talk to you about a trend in recent suicides where the victims shared certain characteristics with the women you killed?"

"I didn't kill them, though, did I? That's why I'm still sitting here, alive, instead of having received a needle in my arm, courtesy of the State of Georgia."

"The jury may not have found a sufficient connection, but I know the truth. You murdered those women."

"No." He shook his head. "I freed them. Just like I freed you."

I bit my lower lip, fighting the urge to argue with him, call him out on being the narcissistic sociopath he was. The more I followed him down whatever rabbit hole he wanted to venture to next, the longer I'd be here. That was the last thing I wanted.

Hardening my expression, I repeated, "Did Claire ask you about recent suicides?"

Nick's eyes bore into mine for several seconds, time seeming to stand still, until he finally relaxed his posture.

"We eventually discussed an unusual trend, but that's not why she originally came to talk to me."

"Then what was her original reason?"

"You already asked one question. It's my turn."

I nodded, crossing my arms in front of my chest as I waited. He chewed on his bottom lip, analytical gaze sweeping over me. I knew this look.

And I didn't like it. Because whatever followed was never good.

At least not for me.

"How many men have you been with?"

This was a test. I'd already admitted I'd been with another man. He wasn't asking in order to get an answer to his question. Instead, it was purely to watch my reaction.

"One."

A smug smile tugged on my mouth when Nick's nostrils flared slightly, lips forming into a tight line. Maybe I should have lied and told him I had an entire harem of men waiting to give me the pleasure he never could. But that wasn't the point of this. Plus, he'd know I was lying.

He always did.

"Now, what was the original reason for Claire's visit?" I crossed my legs and tapped my fingernails against the table, pretending as if my answer didn't just bruise his vastly inflated ego.

He glared at me, his jaw hardening as he attempted to maintain his composure. Then he relaxed.

"She wanted to discuss my background. The early years. She'd hoped to learn a bit more about me in order to do another episode of her podcast. A 'deeper dive', as she called it."

I nodded. "Your turn." I flashed him an unaffected smile.

He tilted his head, intense gaze focused on me. I tried to not let it unnerve me. Reminded myself this was just another part of his game. Another way to take back the upper hand I'd somehow managed to hold onto, despite how uncomfortable I felt being in the same room with him.

"Let's talk about this one person you've been with. How recent was it? Is it still going on?" He glanced at my left hand. "Considering there's no indentation where my ring once sat, it's safe to assume another hasn't yet taken its place. But are you currently involved with this man?"

"I, uh..." His question caught me off guard. I wasn't sure how to answer.

Was I currently involved with Lachlan? Sure, it meant a lot that he came here today to offer me support. But did that fix us?

"It's a yes or no question, Julia," Nick taunted, eyes gleaming with excitement over the prospect of hitting on something he could use to get to me. "You're either still with him or you're not."

"Yes," I answered, although my tone came out hesitant. "It's still going on."

"Are you sure about that? You don't sound certain. What's wrong? Is he unable to give you what you need?"

With every word, he edged closer, the coldness in his

eyes not allowing me to escape. I wanted to tell him I'd never experienced the things Lachlan made me feel. But Nick found his opening. Found my weakness. And he planned to use it against me.

Like he always did.

"Does a brush of his skin against yours light you on fire? Does he make you moan and beg for more? Does he make you come so hard you see stars?"

At the sound of something banging against the two-way mirror, I startled, jumping in my chair.

"Is he here?" Nick's face lit up. "Has he been listening to every word of our conversation?"

"I..."

"Tell me about him, Julia." Licking his lips, he leaned toward me, the malevolence in his stare causing a chill to trickle down my spine. "And don't leave out a single detail."

"I believe I answered your question," I began, voice wavering. "It's my turn."

Nick obviously didn't care about the rules of our game anymore, though, continuing his line of questioning.

"Do you crave his touch? His kiss? His embrace?"

I parted my lips, shaking my head, no words coming.

"Do the hours you're apart seem an interminable curse? Does your heart sing at the mere thought of him?

Do you have dreams of building a life? A home? A family?"

Every word felt like another cut against my skin, a reminder of everything I'd never be able to have because of Nick. Because of what he put me through for years.

"Has he taken my place in your heart? Is he your soul mate? Tell me, Julia... Do you love him?"

"How can I?!"

I shot to my feet, my shrill voice echoing against the walls, all the resolve I struggled to hold onto disappearing in the span of a heartbeat.

"How can I possibly allow him to have a piece of my heart when you fucking destroyed me?! How can I trust anyone enough to have a future with them after you used my trust against me? When every day I woke up scared for my life?! And the life of everyone I cared about?! How can I possibly have a chance at being happy with anyone after what you put me through, you sick, demented fuck?"

The realization of what I'd just confessed suddenly hit me. I clapped my hands over my mouth just as the door flew open, Agent Curran and two guards rushing into the room.

But that wasn't all.

Lachlan stood in the doorway, staring at me, confusion and heartache covering every inch of him.

All I could do was stare, my confession still ringing in the air, taunting and torturing me.

"Let's get you out of here." Agent Curran wrapped an arm around me as Nick's maniacal laughter filled the space.

"And now he knows the truth!" he shouted, his crazed voice victorious. Like this was part of his plan all along.

Lachlan was right.

This was never about sharing what he'd discussed with Claire.

It was to get under my skin.

To exert his power over me.

To manipulate me.

And he did. The fucking bastard did it again.

"He heard firsthand!" Nick continued as the guards dragged him to the door on the other side of the room. "Heard that you still belong to me. That you will *always* belong to me. Like I promised. Till death do us part, Julia. Till death do us part!"

The door slammed closed, causing me to stiffen. As Agent Curran led me from the room, I couldn't stop shaking, Lachlan's heartbroken stare trained on me every step of the way.

"Julia?" He pulled his lip between his teeth, eyes glassy with emotion. "Do you..." He shook his head, swallowing hard. "Do you really believe that? Do you really think we'll never have a chance?"

I peered at him, wanting to tell him I didn't mean any of it. That I didn't believe any of it.

But I couldn't lie.

Instead, I did what I'd done most of my life. I stayed silent as the air grew thick with tension.

"How could I have been so stupid?" he choked out, then pushed past me.

I started after him. "Lachlan, if you'll just—"

He whirled around and advanced, the swift movement startling me.

"Don't," he barked. "Just don't. I can't take any more of your lies or excuses. That's all I've been getting from you for months now. I'm fucking done. And do you want to know the truly upsetting part about this whole thing?"

I swallowed hard past the lump in my throat, tears streaming down my cheeks.

"It's not that you're lying. Or that you keep making excuses. It's the fact you keep lying to yourself. To Imogene. To everyone who fucking loves you. It's..." He trailed off, shaking his head. Then he returned his gaze to mine. "It's sad, Julia. You're sad. I used to think you were this strong, resilient woman who suffered through something so tragic, yet somehow managed to still smile. But now... I don't admire you. I fucking pity you."

His declaration hung heavy in the air, seconds stretching into an eternity, the only sound that of faint footsteps and the occasional buzzing of doors opening and closing.

Then he spun, walking away from me for what I knew in my heart would be the last time.

Nick got what he wanted.

He always did.

CHAPTER TWENTY-SEVEN

Julia

I toyed with my wine glass as I sat in my living room, Naomi on the opposite end of the couch, eyes wide as she struggled to grasp the sad, convoluted tale I'd just shared. I'd kept everything from her for too long. I had my reasons, but I needed someone other than Wes who I could talk to about all of this.

So, the instant I returned from seeing Nick, I called her, instructed her to leave the office and come to my house, where I waited with two large glasses of wine, despite it only being three o'clock in the afternoon. Then I told her everything.

About the jewelry I'd received.

About Claire's podcast and what she was researching.

About her theory that someone was imitating Nick's kill cycle.

How Lachlan was able to confirm that two pieces of jewelry belonged to his former girlfriend and his sister.

How the FBI agent who helped put Nick behind bars all those years ago hoped to reopen some of the local investigations into these women's deaths.

How he was ordered to stand down, forcing Ethan to continue on his own.

How Ethan found a correlation between the locations of these kills and locations where I'd opened branches of my bakery, but had yet to uncover anything definitive.

How Agent Curran looked into Nick's prison visitation records and learned Claire had seen him a dozen times, including the day before her death.

How Agent Curran visited Nick in the hopes of finding out what Claire and he had discussed.

How Nick insisted on seeing me before sharing what they'd talked about.

How Lachlan and I argued over my decision to see Nick.

How it all fell apart.

How much Lachlan's words stung…

Because, deep down, I knew they were true.

I thought I was this strong woman who'd survived something horrendous. In reality, I'd allowed Nick to burrow under my skin again.

If he'd ever left.

I had my doubts.

"Does Imogene know?" Naomi asked in a hushed tone.

I shook my head, sipping my wine. "Not yet. I'm going to tell her. I just..." I trailed off. "I guess I'd hoped Ethan or Agent Curran would uncover something to unequivocally indicate that Nick's connection was purely coincidental."

"And now?" She arched a brow, smoothing her dark hair behind her ear.

I heaved a sigh. "I'm all but certain he's involved in this. He has to be. You should have heard him, Naomi. He was...crazed."

"He's always been crazy," she reminded me. "He was just smart enough to know how to hide it."

"Not like this. It was..." A visible shiver ran through me. "I don't even know. Almost maniacal."

She reached across the couch, grasping my hand. "He can't get to you. And if he somehow does, he'll have me, Wes, and an army of people who care about you to get past this time. He won't win. Trust me on that. He. Will. Not. Win."

I gave her an appreciative smile. After the events of

this past week, this was exactly what I needed. Time with my friend. The reminder that I wasn't alone. Not anymore.

"I guess Lachlan was right after all," I mused as I sagged into the couch. "I *did* play into Nick's hand. Maybe I should have just listened to him and Wes from the beginning."

Naomi tilted her head. "No. I think you made the right call."

"Even knowing it ended in complete disaster?"

"I'm not saying you're entirely free from blame. But neither is Lachlan. You both said and did some things I'm sure you wish you hadn't. But hindsight's twenty-twenty. The present isn't. You made what you thought to be the right decision. Thought visiting Nick could be helpful. But if you look at things from Lachlan's perspective, I understand why he felt like he'd been pushed to his limit. He wakes up to you in the throes of a nightmare where Nick's raping and suffocating you. Knows he has a long record of manipulation, so this could very well just be another game."

"And it was."

Naomi held up a hand. "Not to mention you've been together for over two months now and haven't exactly made any strides toward actually being in a real relationship. The only time you agree to see him is if he comes over to your house or you go over to his." She shook her head. "I warned you a few months ago. That's not quite the best way to be in a relationship."

I closed my eyes, nodding. "I know."

"Then, to make matters worse, he hears you don't think you'll ever be able to open your heart to him, and mere days after he confessed he loved you." She pushed out a disbelieving laugh. "That must have stung. Must have been like someone reached into his chest, yanked out his heart, and presented it to him while it was still beating. And, as we know from experience, when Lachlan's hurt, he lashes out."

"That we do."

"So, while I don't necessarily condone how he behaved and the things he said to you, I can sympathize with his frustration. The entire situation was a powder keg waiting to go off."

"And Nick lit the match."

"I'm afraid he did."

"Hey, Mama?"

I sucked in a breath, darting my eyes toward the kitchen, watching as Imogene hesitantly crept toward us, a hint of concern in her expression.

"Everything okay, baby?" I asked, praying she hadn't overheard our conversation. I'd tried to keep my voice low for that sole purpose.

She plastered on a smile. "I'm going to head over to

Uncle Wes'. Help Eli with some of his footwork for soccer."

"Do you want me to drive you?"

"It's only two streets over. I'll ride my bike."

I paused, not liking the idea of her going out on her own, especially after today. But since we lived in a quiet, family-friendly development with barely any vehicular traffic, I'd allowed her to ride her bike over to her uncle's for years. If I suddenly changed my mind, she'd know something was wrong.

"Text me the second you get there," I told her, using my "mom" voice, as Lachlan called it, which only made my heart squeeze more.

"Of course." She walked toward me, kissing my forehead. "Love you, Mama." She lingered a few beats longer than normal, making me question if maybe she did pick up parts of our conversation.

Then she turned to Naomi, leaning down and giving her a hug. "See ya later, Auntie."

"Love you, kiddo." She kissed her cheek.

Once the front door closed, I faced Naomi again. "So what do I do? The things I said..." I pushed out a sigh. "Not sure those are easily forgotten."

"True. But given the context, they might be better understood."

I furrowed my brows. "What do you mean?"

"How much have you told Lachlan about Nick?"

I averted my gaze, taking a large sip of wine. "He knows enough."

"Which tells me he probably only knows what he could find online and maybe a few additional details here and there."

"I'm trying to put my past behind me," I argued noncommittally.

"Listen to me, Jules."

She grabbed the wine glass from me and set it on the coffee table. Then she took my hands in hers.

"You went through fucking hell with Nick. What the media reported barely skimmed the surface of what living with him did to you. How it changed you. You need to start being honest with Lachlan if you want this to work. Better yet, you need to start being honest with yourself."

"I am—"

"You keep saying how you want to forget the past, put it behind you. I hate to break it to you, but there's not a drug potent enough to help anyone forget the shit Nick put you through. So, instead of pretending like it never happened, it's time you finally embrace it. Celebrate it. Because you fucking survived. Nick tried to beat you down, but he couldn't. Despite everything, he never broke you.

"Let that sink in for a minute, Julia Blaire Prescott. You. Are. Not. Broken."

Her voice punctuated the air, leaving me no choice but to give serious thought to her words.

"Nick may have left a few scars, but that's what makes you the woman you are now. When you got home from Hawaii, you claimed you were done living in survival mode. But you still are. It's time you stop simply surviving and start living. While you're at it, it's time you start loving, too."

I opened my mouth to protest, but she raised her hand again, not allowing me to voice any lackluster arguments.

"I'm not talking about your love for Imogene, Wes, or even me. I'm talking about the soul-fulfilling, heart-bursting love you have for Lachlan. And I know what you're going to say," she added quickly. "That you don't love him. That it's impossible. Well, that's your fear talking."

Her lips twisted into a smile. "When I was dealing with my own relationship struggles, what was it you always mentioned your meemaw said? About how I'd know it was love?"

I closed my eyes, almost able to feel my grandmother's arms around me as she tried to explain something as mysterious and frightening as love.

"'If you're not scared, it's not love.'"

"Precisely. So let me ask you this..."

I slowly lifted my gaze to meet Naomi's.

"How do you feel right now?"

"Petrified."

She smirked. "That's what I thought. I'm not saying telling him the truth will fix everything. But I think he deserves to know your true feelings. Stop trying to protect him. Better yet, stop trying to protect yourself. Stop living in survival mode and fucking *live*, Jules."

CHAPTER TWENTY-EIGHT

Lachlan

I stared at the rocks glass sitting on the coffee table, the scotch I'd poured barely touched. I'd wanted something to help dull the sting from Julia's words. But I doubted anything could ever ease the pain from hearing her say she'd never be able to give me her heart.

That she'd never love me.

That Nick would always have his claws in her.

Since returning from the prison hours ago, Julia's words had continually replayed in my mind, causing my anger and frustration to increase with each repetition.

And with each repetition, my need to dull the pain grew stronger. Hitting my breaking point, I reached for my glass, about down the scotch when the doorbell rang.

I opened the doorbell app on my phone, jumping to my feet when I saw Imogene standing there, her bike leaning against my porch railing.

Dread snaked through me as I darted to the front door, flinging it wide, my panicked expression meeting hers.

"Imogene, what's wrong?"

"Nothing." She shrugged, shoving her hands into her pockets, a nervousness about her.

"Are you okay?"

My gaze raked over her, making sure she *was* okay after riding her bike all the way here, which I knew for a fact her mother would kill her for.

"I'm fine."

"And your mum?" I asked, unsure how much Imogene knew about what happened today. Not only the fact that Julia had gone to see Nick, but also about our argument.

And the things I'd said.

"She's...okay."

"Okay." I pushed out a relieved breath. "Then what—"

"I know she went to see him today," she blurted.

"You do?"

"Auntie Naomi came over this afternoon. As I'm sure you're aware, she's not exactly...soft-spoken." She snorted a subtle laugh.

I shook my head, chuckling. "She's certainly not." I stepped back, pulling the door wide. "Come on in."

"Thanks." She gave me a small smile as she entered.

A smile that was nearly identical to her mother's, regardless of what that narcissistic sociopath wanted to believe. When I looked at Imogene, I didn't see any piece of that bastard. She had her mother's influence all over her.

Not her father's.

"Want something to drink? Water? Coffee? Whatever it is fourteen-year-old kids drink?"

She rolled her eyes, her attitude peeking through. "Water's fine."

I headed into the kitchen and grabbed a bottle from the fridge, handing it to her.

"So, want to tell me why you're here?" I asked.

She parted her lips, that same contemplative look Julia often got crossing her expression. "Mama hasn't told you a lot about...before, has she?"

I briefly sucked in a breath, unsure what to tell her. What Julia would want me to tell her. But I wasn't going to lie.

"I know...broad strokes."

"But no details?"

I slowly shook my head. "No details."

Nodding, as if she'd expected that answer, she spun, walking across the dark brown wood flooring and to the expansive windows overlooking my back yard. I followed, albeit hesitantly, gauging her demeanor.

In the span of a heartbeat, the normal teenage girl transitioned into someone who appeared so much more mature.

So much more jaded.

"We used to play hide-and-seek a lot."

"You and your mum?"

She lifted her eyes to mine, giving me a subtle shake of her head before peering out the windows once more.

With that one gesture, a chill washed over me. I didn't have to ask to know about whom she was referring. The distance in her stare said it all.

"Whenever Mama excused herself from whatever we were doing, whether it was shopping, swimming at the community pool, or walking around the county fair, he'd want to play." She pinned me with a look. "Without telling her."

My jaw tensed, blood boiling in my veins.

"He'd grab me and hide us out of view. I was young, but it felt wrong. So many times, I wanted to cry out for Mama, tell her where we were. But I was scared of what he'd do to her if I did. So I stayed quiet."

"And what would happen?"

"He'd play his game." She looked forward, as if watching a movie playing before her eyes.

Memories no little girl should have had to endure.

"He'd have this strange look on his face as he watched Mama panic. And not just a little panic, like you did earlier when you saw me at your front door. This was a full-fledged panic attack. Crying, screaming, begging anyone to help her find me. And through it all, he kept his hand over my mouth, hushing me if I made so much as a whimper. When he did reappear with me, he'd make it sound like she wasn't right in the head. That he'd told her where we went. That her reaction was completely unwarranted. It made her doubt her own sanity."

My nostrils flared as I clenched and unclenched my fists, fighting the urge to punch a wall. I refused to show Imogene anything remotely resembling violence, though.

It was one thing to listen to Julia talk about Nick's ability to manipulate. But to listen to Imogene recall her memories of some of the twisted games he played made me wild with rage.

Made me want revenge, regardless of the price I'd pay to get it.

"I was too young to fully understand, but I do now. I know why he did it. Not to scare her or force her to make a scene..."

"To control her," I breathed.

Imogene nodded. "Everything he did was to control her. To remind her of the power he held. To remind her if she stepped out of line, that if she even thought about leaving him, he'd take away the one thing she cared about most in this world." She smiled sadly. "Me."

"I want to kill him," I seethed before I could stop the words from leaving my mouth. "I'm sorry, Imogene. I know he's your father, but—"

"Wrong," she interjected, glaring over her shoulder at me. "He's my *sperm donor.*" Her words came out with a determination I doubted I had at her age. "He lost the right to consider himself my father before I was even born."

She floated her gaze out the window once more, focusing on the reflection of the sun in my pool.

"Mama's always shielded me from everything to do with him. Maybe she thought if she did, I wouldn't remember how bad it was. I may not remember everything, but I haven't forgotten his games." She swept her eyes back to mine, tilting her head. "But despite all that, do you know what memory stands out amongst them all?"

"What's that?"

"At night, after he'd play one of his games, Mama would always sneak into my room, crawl into bed with me, hold me close, and sing."

"What did she sing?"

Tears welled in her eyes. "'Smile'."

"'Smile'?"

Facing forward again, Imogene began to sing. I

instantly knew the song, the lyrics about putting on a smile even though your life was pretty much falling apart around you. The exact thing I had a feeling Julia had done her entire life.

"I think it was her way of convincing herself it was all worth it. Her way of reminding me that we were stronger than him. That one day we'd *show* him we were stronger than he was. That he may have won the battle, but he wouldn't win the war."

She faced me again. "And just like his purpose of hide-and-seek wasn't for Mama to find us, the purpose of his game today wasn't to find out information."

I furrowed my brows. "It wasn't?"

"Nick doesn't ask questions he doesn't already know the answer to. So for everything he asked her today, he already knew the answer. Instead, he asked them—"

"To see how she would react," I interjected with a sigh.

"Not just her. But you, too."

I hung my head, running a hand over my face. "And I played right into his hand."

"You both did. Doesn't mean it's too late to try again."

I narrowed my gaze on her. "I said some really ugly things. Called her sad. Said I pitied her."

"Because she told you she'd never be able to let you into her heart, which hurt...because you love her."

"You heard that?"

She shrugged. "The first part. I figured out the second part on my own."

"What part is that?"

"That you love her. And deep down, I know she loves you, too. And I'm not just saying that because you're Lachlan Hale and you play for my favorite baseball team." She smiled before her expression sobered again. "I'm saying that because I think you're good for her. Since you've come into her life, she's been...happy. That may not seem like a big deal to most people, but for my mama, it's huge. She's just really stubborn. And scared. She's been through a lot."

"As have you."

"Not like her," she declared vehemently. "She's done everything to make sure that stuff didn't affect me, often at the expense of her own happiness. And maybe that's why she doesn't think she can ever trust or love you. Because my sperm donor has a history of using her love and trust against her at every turn. Just... Don't give up on her."

"I could never give up on your mum," I admitted with a sigh. "But I'm not sure she'll ever forgive the things I said."

She smirked, expression lightening. "I hear groveling can be effective. And jewelry." She cringed. "Actually, no. Pretty sure Mama never wants to receive jewelry as a gift for the rest of her life."

I chuckled, grateful for the break in tension. All thanks to this unassuming fourteen-year-old.

"You're probably right about that."

"Then cupcakes." Imogene nodded. "Groveling and cupcakes."

"Cupcakes? But she's a pastry chef."

"You know what she always says, don't you?"

"What's that?"

"It's impossible to be angry when holding a cupcake."

Recognition flashed in my brain. "That's on the wall of her bakery in Buckhead."

"Yes, it is."

I expelled a long breath. "Okay, kid. Here's what we're going to do. First, I'm going to call your mum to tell her you're over here and are safe."

Her expression fell as she groaned. "Do you have to? She's going to be pissed. I told her I was going over to my uncle Wes' house, since I knew she'd never let me ride all the way out here on my own."

"And for good reason." I crossed my arms in front of my chest, giving her a stern look. "You crossed several busy intersections. All it would have taken was one shit-head texting while driving and that would have been it.

If anything happens to you, it would destroy her, Imogene."

Giving me an annoyed glare, she held out her hand. "That'll be five dollars."

"For what?"

"Swearing."

"Your mum only gives you a dollar."

"My mom doesn't have a five-year, $100 million contract pitching for one of the best professional base-ball teams around right now. You can afford it, Hale."

I mumbled, but reached into my pocket and opened my wallet. "Lowest I've got is a twenty. Got any change?"

She grabbed the bill out of my hand, shoving it into her back pocket. "Let's call it even. So, what's the plan after you tattle on me?"

"You know how to bake, right?"

She scoffed. "Of course I know how to bake."

"Good. Because I'm going to need your help."

"I'll say."

CHAPTER TWENTY-NINE

Julia

The second the front door opened, I jumped up from the couch and bolted toward the foyer, eyes on fire. I'd never been so angry at Imogene in my life.

She'd lied to me. Rode her bike five miles through the busy Atlanta streets. Intruded on Lachlan.

I could only imagine what he must have thought when Imogene showed up on his doorstep without my knowledge.

Then again, he did offer to feed her dinner since he thought I could use a break.

And I could. I just didn't know from what.

As Imogene's eyes met mine, I opened my mouth, about to chastise her behavior and ground her until she

turned eighteen. But when Lachlan stepped up behind
her, a plastic storage container in his hands, I snapped
my jaw shut. I knew he was driving her home. He'd said
as much when he'd called to inform me she was at his
house.

I just hadn't anticipated he'd walk her *into* the
house.

Didn't think he'd want to see me after everything.

But as I studied his face, there wasn't so much as a
hint of the anger that consumed him earlier. Instead, his
eyes were awash with remorse.

"Don't be mad at him," Imogene said before I could
utter a word. "You can't be mad. Not right now. Not
about this. See." She yanked the container from his hand
and tilted it toward me. "He made you cupcakes.
Remember what you always say…"

I pushed out a long sigh, pinching the bridge of my
nose. "It's impossible to be angry when holding a
cupcake."

"Exactly."

She proceeded into the house, setting it onto the
kitchen island, while we remained in the foyer, neither
of us saying anything. I wasn't sure what *to* say, my mind
still processing not only everything I'd admitted at the
prison earlier today, but also what Naomi told me this
afternoon.

When Imogene returned, she grabbed my hand and placed a cupcake in it, then did the same to Lachlan.

"Now you're both holding cupcakes. So you *can't* be angry." She pointed at me. "*You* can't be angry at him for what he said." She spun, shoving her finger into Lachlan's chest. "And *you* can't be mad at her for what she said."

I floated my gaze down to the treat in my hand, the familiar scent of cinnamon, nutmeg, and sugar invading my senses. A smile tugged on my lips from the memories this tasty treat conjured. At one time, it would only evoke memories of spending time in Meemaw's kitchen.

Now all I could think of as I stared at the cupcake version of my hummingbird cake was Lachlan and our first night together in Hawaii.

"You made me hummingbird cupcakes?"

He gave me a sheepish smile. "I did."

Imogene cleared her throat dramatically.

"Imogene helped," Lachlan said with a proud gleam. "She's really quite remarkable."

I looked her way, eyes filling with affection. "She truly is."

"Okay." Imogene glanced between the two of us. "Now that you both have cupcakes, you can talk about all this nonsense like two civilized, *un-angry* human beings. Right?"

We both nodded simultaneously.

"Right," I agreed.

"Of course," Lachlan said, his gaze not straying from mine, a thousand apologies written within.

"Good. I'm going to hold you both to that." She pinned us with a glare. Then she spun on her heels, darting up the stairs.

"You're not off the hook, young lady!" I called after her.

"Yes, I am!" she sang back.

"No, you're not!" I yelled just as her door closed.

Then I exhaled a breath, shaking my head. "Who am I kidding? Of course she is."

"Any reason for that?"

I felt Lachlan inch toward me before I heard his voice. Lifting my eyes to see he was only a breath away, all I could do was shrug.

"She brought you back to me."

He reached for a tendril of hair, pushing it behind my ear. "I'll always come back for you, Julia."

His gaze bore into mine for several moments, allowing his promise to sink in.

"And, technically, the cupcakes brought you back to me."

I laughed, averting my eyes. "I never could say no to a cupcake."

"Neither could I."

I glanced between our hands, each of us still holding

a cupcake. If anyone walked in and saw us standing like this, they'd probably think it strange.

For us, though, it was perfect.

"Can we talk?" he asked timidly, as if waiting for me to turn him away because of all the hurtful things we'd said to each other.

"I'd like that."

Cupcake in hand, I led him toward the couch and lowered myself onto one end as he sat a few feet away. Still close enough for me to smell his delicious scent, but a bit farther away than he'd normally be.

"Do we still have to hold these?" He lifted his cupcake. "Is she going to yell at us if she learns we set them down?"

"She might. After all, she *is* my daughter. She can be quite willful and headstrong."

He nodded, blowing out a subtle laugh under his breath. "She certainly can be. It's one of the things I love about her." He swallowed hard. "That I love about you."

My throat constricted at how easily he admitted it, despite everything that had transpired today. He made it appear so effortless, but I knew the truth. Knew how scared he was of giving someone else his heart after everything he'd lost.

Yet he didn't let that stop him from giving me his heart.

And I had a feeling he'd continue giving it to me,

regardless of whether I accepted it. Love didn't stop just because we willed it to. Some forces were outside our control.

Meeting Lachlan taught me that.

He set his cupcake on the coffee table, then grabbed mine, placing it beside his. When he faced me again, we both spoke at the same time.

"Listen, Julia—"

"Lachlan, I—"

We stopped short, then laughed nervously.

"Normally, I'd do the gentlemanly thing and say ladies first..." He ran his fingers through his hair, "but not right now. I owe you an apology. In truth, I owe you more than just an apology, but it's all I have."

I nodded toward the table. "You did make me cupcakes."

"True. But even cupcakes are a shite consolation prize, considering how badly I fucked up today. And that's the truth of it. I. Fucked. Up. I was a daft prick. The things I said to you, the things I called you..." He shook his head sadly. "That's not who I am. Sure, I can be a hothead sometimes, and I own that. But after the strength you showed by facing your own personal demon today..." He swallowed hard. "I should have supported you. Should have shown you compassion. Shown you love. Instead, I did the exact opposite. I did what I knew would hurt you the most." He raised his anguished eyes to mine. "I was no better than him."

"You're *nothing* like him." I grabbed his hands, the feeling of his flesh against mine comforting. "You must believe that. You've shown me compassion every day since we met." I cupped his cheek, savoring in the scruffiness of his unshaven jawline. "You've shown me love every day since we met. Nick wouldn't even know the meaning of the word. All he knows is control and manipulation."

He pinched his lips into a tight line, a contemplative look furrowing his brows. Then he declared, "Imogene told me about the game he used to play."

I pulled away, a chill rushing through me. "Game?"

"Hide-and-seek."

"What did..." I swallowed hard. "What did she tell you about it?"

His jaw twitched, vein throbbing in his neck. He quickly picked up his cupcake, closing his eyes as he drew in several deep breaths.

Something about the image of Lachlan Hale, all six-four and impressive muscle, holding a cupcake to suppress his anger endeared him to me even more.

Despite my insistence earlier today that I'd never be able to allow anyone into my heart.

But I had months ago.

I knew it.

Lachlan knew it.

And, best of all, Nick knew it.

"Imogene mentioned he'd make her hide from you just to see your reaction. To terrify you."

I should have known Imogene would remember more than I'd hoped. She was young when Nick's crimes made headlines. But the memories she did have were the foundation of her childhood. She may not recall the tiny details, but she remembered the big picture.

And this game was most certainly the big picture.

"She knew what he was doing hurt you, but she was too scared to say anything."

He blew out a small laugh, shaking his head in disbelief. "It took a fourteen-year-old kid for me to realize what really happened today. The purpose of all those questions. I was so angry at you for not seeing this was just a way for him to manipulate you that I didn't see the truth."

"And what truth is that?"

"That I played right into his hand, too. Imogene said something that hit me."

"She did?"

He nodded. "She said Nick doesn't ask any question he doesn't already know the answer to. So his little game earlier... It was his way of trying to manipulate you. To push you to your breaking point so you'd snap." His

Adam's apple bobbed up and down in a hard swallow. "And me."

I whipped my eyes to meet his. "What?"

"It was his way of trying to manipulate *me*, too. To push *me* to my breaking point so I'd snap."

He set his cupcake back down and held my hands in his. "Do you remember what you used to do at night when Imogene was little? After he played one of his games?"

I nodded, blinking back my tears. "I'd always crawl into her bed."

"And what song would you sing to her?"

I choked out a sob at the fact she remembered. "'Smile'."

"Exactly. So consider this my version of crawling into bed with you and trying to assure you that, no matter what that bastard attempts to throw at us, I'm not going to give up on you. On us. That's what he wants. He may have won the battle today..." He moved his hands to my face, "but I'll be damned if I'm going to stand by and let him win the war."

"I shouldn't have said—"

He shook his head, cutting me off. "Who cares if you don't think you can trust anyone right now? Or give anyone a piece of your heart? I've never backed down from a challenge. And I won't back down from this one, either. Even if it takes me every day for the rest of my life, I'm going to prove to you that there *are* good people in the world. And that, even though I may have my faults, I'm one of them. That you *can* trust me. And maybe, in time, that you can love me, too."

He brought my face closer to his, his breath warming my lips. "I'm so bloody sorry for what I said," he murmured against me. "Please, Julia... Let's start again."

"Start again?"

Clearing his throat, he dropped his hold on me and increased the distance between us, gaze locked on mine.

"My name is Lachlan Hale. My favorite things are making breakfast for you and your daughter, coming home to you after a tough game, and that thing you do with your tongue on my earlobe. Oh, and phone sex." He winked. "Can't forget about that."

"Certainly not," I laughed as I swiped away my tears, all the anxiety that had plagued me since walking into the prison disappearing now that we'd taken that first step in clearing the air.

Now that Lachlan had a better picture of what life with Nick was really like.

"And even though you can be so bloody stubborn sometimes," he continued before sobering, eyes gleaming with affection, "I'm completely in love with you, Julia Blaire Prescott."

The mood instantly shifted, his stare unwavering as his confession hung in the air. He didn't attempt to hide from it. Instead, he laid himself bare for me. Allowed himself to be vulnerable, even though I knew it petrified him.

"So there you have it. That's me. Take it or leave it."

I briefly closed my eyes as I drew in a shaky breath, attempting to collect my thoughts. Then I fixed my gaze on Lachlan, his blue orbs filled with so much love.

I felt a crack form in the hard exterior I'd erected years ago when I didn't think I had any other choice but to keep people out in order to protect myself.

"My name's Julia Prescott," I began with a smile. "My favorite things in the world are having breakfast with you and Imogene, feeling you crawl into bed beside me after a long day, and that thing *you* do with your tongue on my earlobe. Oh, and phone sex. Can't forget about that."

"Never. I'll be a senile old man and will still remember the sounds you make when you come."

My face heated, lips twisting into a smile. I'd remember the way Lachlan made me feel until I was old and senile, too.

When I lifted my gaze back to his, I summoned all the courage I possessed to face my biggest fear.

"And I'm completely in love with you, Lachlan Keone Hale."

He blinked repeatedly, jaw dropping. "What— What did you just say?"

"That I love you," I repeated, as if it were the easiest thing in the world. The truth was, it *was* easy to say it.

"But—"

"Earlier today, I didn't believe I'd ever be able to let anyone into my heart, especially when I was in that room with Nick." I clutched his hands, holding them tightly. "But I love you, Lachlan. Love how you love me, even when I can be a giant pain in the ass. Or, as you say it, *arse*."

"And I thought you liked my Australian accent." He winked.

"That I do. In fact, I love it. And I love how incredible you are with Imogene. How you constantly keep me on my toes." I placed my hand over his heart. "Mostly, I love how you've made room in here for me, even after all the shit you've been through. I can't promise things will always be easy. That I won't do things that drive you absolutely crazy."

"I'm counting on you pissing me off on a regular basis. My mum often said that loving someone doesn't mean you always get along or never have an argument. It means that, despite the bad days, you can't imagine your life without them in it."

"And I cannot imagine living a single day of my life without you in it, Lachlan Hale. You're...a part of me." I took his hand and placed it over my heart. "You own this. Completely. It's yours... If you'll have it."

I held his gaze for several protracted moments. Then I pulled back.

"So there you have it. That's me. Take it or leave it."

He didn't hesitate, yanking my body against his. "Take. I absolutely fucking take."

Digging his fingers into my cheeks, he crushed his lips to mine, coaxing them open, a warmth building in my heart and spreading throughout my body. When his tongue swept against mine, I sighed, melting into his kiss, his taste, his everything.

Our love didn't hit me suddenly, stealing my breath and arresting my heart. Instead, it crept in slowly. A touch here. A kind word there. But with each compassionate gesture, Lachlan had managed to dismantle the walls I'd erected around my heart until I didn't know where mine ended and his began.

For too long, I was scared to admit what this feeling truly was. But now I knew.

And I wasn't going to run from love anymore.

I wasn't going to be *scared* of love anymore.

Love made us stronger.

And I had to believe it would make us strong enough to get through whatever the future held.

CHAPTER THIRTY

Julia

The early morning sun filtered into my bedroom, stirring me from a restful sleep, something I hadn't enjoyed in nearly a week. Not since Agent Curran's visit.

It was remarkable how different the world seemed now that I finally took a leap of faith. Finally allowed love into my heart.

Finally allowed my heart to love in return.

An arm snaked around my torso, pulling me close.

"I can hear you thinking," Lachlan mused in a raspy voice.

I laughed slightly.

I'd lost count of the number of times we had this

same conversation first thing in the morning. Such an insignificant, mundane part of our day.

But one of the many things that helped chip away at the wall around my heart.

"You can hear me thinking?"

"I can." He peppered soft kisses along my shoulder blade, the gesture comforting, addicting.

"Then pray tell, Mr. Hale..." I shifted in the bed to face him.

When I threaded my fingers through his hair, he closed his eyes, basking in my touch. I inched my lips toward his, remaining a breath away.

"What am I thinking?"

"It doesn't work that way." His deep voice was laden with desire. "I can't hear *what* you're thinking. Just that you are."

"Well then..." Pressing a hand to his chest, I forced him onto his back and crawled on top of him, straddling his waist. I circled my hips, my lips brushing his. "Let me *show* you what I was thinking."

Lifting myself up slightly, I wrapped my hand around his erection, guiding him inside me, his arousal filling me inch by glorious inch.

"I really like what you were thinking," he groaned, pulling me toward him, digging his fingers into my hair.

"I thought you might," I mused just before he sealed his mouth over mine, tongues tangling as I moved against him, a dizzying current rushing through me.

"I bloody love what you were thinking. Love the way you move." He cupped my face in his hands, not allowing me to look away. "I love you, Julia."

My heart swelled in response to those three little words. But they weren't just three words said out of duty or obligation, as I sensed was the case most of my life. But I physically felt the love this man had for me radiating through every inch of him. There was nothing fake or forced about it. It was real.

Probably the most real thing I'd ever experienced.

Bringing my lips back to his, I murmured, "And I love you, Lachlan."

He sighed, touching his mouth to mine as I pulsed against him, chasing that sensation of bliss he'd spoiled me with multiple times last night. But with Lachlan, I always needed more. More of him. More of this euphoria. More of his love.

"I will never get tired of hearing you say that, beautiful." He moved his hands to my hips and guided my motions, his own thrusts turning intense and demanding. "And I will never get tired of showing you how much I love you." He brought a hand back to my head, pulling my mouth toward his. "How much you mean to me, love."

"Oh god," I moaned as his lips brushed mine, the

combination of his words and the way he moved inside me pushing me higher and higher until I couldn't fight it any longer, fireworks erupting in my core.

He pulled me close, swallowing my cries as he drove into me a few more times before he stiffened, succumbing to his own desires, our heavy breathing puncturing an otherwise peaceful morning.

I collapsed on top of him, basking in the warmth of his arms around me, comforting me. Reassuring me. Protecting me.

Loving me.

"Come to California with me today," he murmured as he kissed the top of my head, his hands caressing my sweat-dotted back.

I peered up into his eyes, a twinge of hope within. But also a hint of resignation, as if fully expecting me to give him the same response I always did.

But things were different now. I was done being a pawn in whatever game Nick was playing.

Months ago, I'd claimed I was ready to jump.

It was time to finally prove it.

I brushed my mouth against his. "Yes."

He sucked in a breath, eyes widening. "Yes?" he repeated, unsure he'd heard me correctly.

I nodded, biting my lower lip in an attempt to reel in my smile. "Yes, Lachlan. I will come to California with you."

"People might see us. I flew commercial back here from California on a red-eye Thursday night after my game so I could be there for you yesterday. I'd planned on flying commercial back, too. I could try to arrange a charter, but—"

I placed a finger over his lips, silencing him. "Let them see us. Let the world see us together. I'm done hiding what we have." I frowned. "As long as you're okay with this. I'm sure—"

Before I could utter another syllable, his mouth covered mine, tongue teasing mine in a kiss I felt everywhere.

Including my heart.

"I'm *more* than okay with this. If you recall, I've been waiting for this day for quite some time now."

"Yes, you have." I waggled my brows. "I think you deserve a reward for your patience. Wouldn't you agree?"

A mischievous glint in my eyes, I slid down his body, his erection hardening again the instant I wrapped my fingers around it.

"What kind of reward did you have in mind?" He rested his hands behind his head, the picture of relaxation.

"Let me show you."

I brought my mouth to his tip, about to drag my tongue along his length, when the doorbell rang.

"Jesus, Mary, and all that is holy," Lachlan groaned, squeezing his eyes shut. "You've *got* to be kidding me."

Hesitating, I considered ignoring whomever it was. But it *was* barely eight in the morning. I had a feeling whatever the reason for someone showing up this early on a Saturday had to be important.

"Let me just see who it is." I leaned over him, draping my body along his as I reached for my phone on the nightstand.

"And tell them to bugger off so you can suck my cock."

I laughed, playfully swatting him as he ran a hand up my thigh. "Such a gentleman."

"I never purported to be one, love. In fact..." He thrust against me. "I'm pretty sure you prefer it when I'm *not* a gentleman."

I glanced over my shoulder at the heat in his gaze. "You know I do." I held his stare for a moment, then returned my attention to the phone.

When I opened the doorbell feed, I scrambled off Lachlan and shot to sitting.

"Who is it?" he asked, leaning over my shoulder and peering at the screen.

"Ethan."

He squinted, watching as Ethan paced my front porch, hair disheveled, shirt wrinkled. Completely out of character for a man who was always clean-cut and organized, his attire ordinarily impeccable.

"I'm going to throttle that cockblocker."

"Can you wait until *after* he tells us why he's here? It might be important."

"I'll try my best."

"Thank you."

I stood, about to head to the dresser to throw on some clothes, when Lachlan looped his arm around me, pulling me back onto the bed.

"Don't think I'm letting you off the hook. You promised to suck me off. And I expect you to fulfill your end of the bargain."

I pinched my lips together. "Did I promise, though? I don't believe I actually said, 'Lachlan, I vow to suck you off.'"

"That's the beauty about being in professional sports as long as I have. I've gotten quite familiar with contracts. Did you know that, even in the absence of express language, an offer can be inferred if an individual implies a readiness to perform a certain act?"

"Is that right?"

"The way I heard it, you absolutely implied a readiness to suck my cock." He threaded his fingers through my hair. "And I absolutely accept that offer. One hundred fucking percent, beautiful."

I threw my head back, laughing. After yesterday, it

felt good to joke around with him. Felt good to be happy again.

The doorbell rang once more.

"Okay, you fiend." I swatted him away. "Let's go see what Ethan wants so we can come back up here and fulfill this 'contract'."

"Now you're talking."

CHAPTER THIRTY-ONE

Lachlan

"I'm glad you're both here," Ethan said the second I answered Julia's door.

He barreled into the house, everything about him agitated, a complete one-eighty from his usual put-together appearance. His eyes were bloodshot, blond hair sticking up every which way. It looked like he hadn't slept in days.

"We need to talk." He headed straight to the kitchen island, dropping a large, expandable folder on top of it with a thump.

"Can I get you anything?" Julia eyed him warily. "Maybe water, since it looks like you've had plenty of caffeine?" She glanced at his trembling hand as he pulled a stack of papers out of the folder.

"I'm fine. I just..." He paused, drawing in a deep breath. "I think I'm on to something."

"What's that?" Julia slid onto the barstool beside him.

"Coffee?" I murmured against her cheek.

She gave me a quick nod, then returned her attention to Ethan.

"Since Agent Curran said not much came out of yesterday's...meeting..." He offered Julia a sympathetic smile, "I spent all afternoon going through Claire's research, hunting for the proverbial needle in the haystack. Her system is, well... The only word I can think of is chaos. Not even *organized* chaos. Just boxes upon boxes of stuff in no discernible order. While it may have made sense to her, it's made trying to figure out what she was looking into nearly impossible."

"So you *didn't* find anything?" Julia asked as I placed a mug in front of her. Then I sat on the other side of her.

"I said *nearly* impossible."

With a grin, Ethan tossed what appeared to be a dorm incident report onto the island.

"What's this?" Julia picked up the sheets.

"I have no idea how Claire got this, but she'd apparently started looking into reports of rape or sexual assault on and around the various college campuses where Nick attended undergraduate and graduate school."

"Why?"

"She obviously had a hunch. One she didn't share with me. But it makes sense. Would explain why she visited Nick and wanted to talk to him about his younger years."

"What makes sense?" I pressed.

"Julia wasn't his first victim. This woman was." He pulled a photo out of his file and placed it onto the island.

I blinked repeatedly, shaking my head. "I think you're confused, Ethan. That's Lucy Shea. One of the team's owners."

He nodded slowly. "When she attended Brown for undergrad, she met Domenic Jaskulski, which was where he received his first PhD at the age of twenty. Notice anything interesting about her statement to the RA of her dorm?"

Julia and I scanned the brief report, the contents all too familiar.

One spring night, Lucy Shea, who was still Lucy Ellis at the time, went to Open Mic Night at a nearby coffee shop. She started to feel lightheaded and thought perhaps she was coming down with something, so she left early, walking the few blocks to her on-campus apartment. She couldn't remember much after that. The next thing she knew, she woke up and it was morning.

And there was blood between her legs.

"Did anything come of this?" I asked, although I already had a feeling what the answer would be.

"Depends on how you look at it." Ethan smirked, a victorious expression on his face.

Julia leaned toward him, eyes determined. "What do you mean?"

"Were criminal charges ever filed? I think we all know the answer to that." He gave us a knowing look. Then he smiled slyly. "But something *did* come of it. Approximately two months later, Lucy Ellis became Lucy Shea. And seven months later, a healthy baby boy was born."

He tossed a photo of Daxton onto the surface. But he didn't stop there. He then produced what looked to be a photograph of Nick during his twenties and placed it beside a current one of Dax.

"This is all conjecture, but I find the resemblance quite remarkable. Don't you?"

I shot my gaze to Julia, wondering how she'd handle the surprising news, but I appeared more shocked by this than she did.

"I always thought he might have more children out there." She shrugged. "If you're going around sticking your dick into everything with a pulse, like a modern-day Zeus, you'd think you'd at least wrap it up. Then again, Zeus didn't, either."

I ran my hand up and down her back in a soothing gesture as I returned my gaze to Ethan.

"While this is certainly interesting, it doesn't prove anything. It's suspicious, but just because Dax *may* be Nick's biological child doesn't mean he's involved in what's currently going on. Hell, based on that rationale, Imogene should be a suspect, too."

"You're right. The fact they may share DNA doesn't prove anything. But I have something that might."

He sifted through the folder and pulled out another photograph, setting it in front of us. "Remember her?"

Julia nodded, eyes trained on the young, vivacious brunette in the picture. "Autumn Quinn. The Emory student who volunteered for Homes for the Homeless. Was murdered five years ago this past March, if our theory's to be believed."

"Exactly." Ethan reached into his folder and placed yet another photo onto the island. "Now, take a look at this picture I lifted off her social media tribute account. Anything look familiar? Or perhaps should I say anyone?"

Julia and I leaned closer, staring at the grainy photo taken in dim lighting. Obviously a bar.

But despite the low lighting, the people in the photo were unmistakable, Autumn's smile bright as she beamed at the camera. And beside her, his lips pressed to her cheek, stood Dax.

But that wasn't all. She wore a Celtic cross necklace I easily recognized.

As did Julia.

"When was this taken?" she asked, her surprise evident.

"A week before her death."

"Is he... Do you think he's behind this?"

"Again, while suspicious, the fact it appears he dated Autumn Quinn at the time of her death doesn't mean anything. So I did even more digging. Do you want to know what I found?"

Neither Julia nor I said anything, simply staring at Ethan.

"All the 'suicides' that occurred outside this guy's comfort zone, with the exception of Piper, took place when your team was on the road. And in those precise locations. Does Daxton travel with the team often?"

I slowly nodded, heat washing over me.

I'd always liked Dax. Sure, when I first met him, I didn't think much of him. He was my age, a bit geeky. But over the past few years, as his parents slowly put more responsibilities on his shoulders, he seemed to really come into his own. I still had trouble wrapping my mind around the idea that he could have been responsible for something like this.

Then again, wasn't that what people often said about Ted Bundy?

"Not to *all* the away games, but he does go to some. He's passionate about the game, even if he can't hit worth a lick."

"I believe he goes to those away games for this precise reason."

"Jesus Christ." I ran a hand over my face, not wanting to believe it. But the more I thought of everything I knew, the more the puzzle pieces snapped into place.

After the injuries I suffered as a result of the home invasion, Dax had pushed for management to keep me on the roster. He'd even flown out to Hawaii to visit me in the hospital.

Or maybe he was already *in* Hawaii.

My stomach churned.

"That's not all," Ethan said.

"There's more?" I asked through the frustration and rage forming a knot in my throat, fists clenching, muscles tense.

Julia grabbed my hand, giving it a reassuring squeeze.

Ethan hesitated, glancing between me and Julia. "The Prison Outreach program Nick's been participating in? The one that's allowed him to receive regular visits from a clergy member?"

"Yes?" My voice came out strained.

"Daxton Shea is a volunteer."

CHAPTER THIRTY-TWO

Julia

"I'm going to kill him." Lachlan's voice was eerily calm as he stared into space. "But first, I'm going to make him suffer for every woman he hurt. For Piper. For Claire. For all of them. By the time I'm done with him, he's going to be begging me to put him out of his misery."

"Lachlan..."

When I placed my hand on his leg, his gaze shot to mine, snapping out of whatever trance he was in.

"It could be nothing, like Ethan said." I flashed Ethan a smile, begging him to help me talk Lachlan down from choosing a course of action he'd eventually come to regret. "There's nothing definitive here. So what? Daxton was born only seven months after his parents married. Nine months after his mother filed an incident report alleging sexual assault."

"Sexual assault that has your ex-husband's signature all over it," Lachlan snipped back.

"True." I inhaled a calming breath, attempting to be the voice of reason when it felt like all reason had officially left the room. "But that still doesn't mean—"

"And how about the fact he obviously knew Autumn Quinn?" he spat, nostrils flaring, spittle forming in the corners of his mouth. "Is that also a coincidence? Not to mention he just so happens to volunteer for a fucking prison program and has had access to your ex. Is *that* all a coincidence, too?"

Hearing footsteps padding on the second floor, I glanced over my shoulder at the stairs before refocusing my attention on Lachlan, lowering my voice. "Please keep it down. For Imogene. She can't know about this. Not yet."

He squeezed his eyes shut, digging his fingers through his hair. "I introduced them."

"Who?"

"Dax and Piper. And Claire." He laughed to himself. "I should have—"

"We still don't know anything for certain." I held his gaze for a moment before facing Ethan again.

"With this new...development, is that enough to

involve the FBI? Or, at the very least, reopen the investigation into Claire's death? And perhaps Autumn's?" I gestured to her photo.

"I put a call into Agent Curran this morning and am waiting to hear back. I'm sure he'll be of the same mindset we are." Ethan glanced at Lachlan. "That it *is* suspicious."

"Damn straight it is," he growled.

"Still... Whatever we do, we need to be delicate about this."

Ethan looked toward the front windows as sirens blared in the distance. It was strange to hear them this far out in the suburbs. Then again, as I'd learned, bad shit could happen anywhere.

"Daxton isn't your run-of-the-mill criminal. If he *is* the one behind this, he's gotten away with it for five years now. And with his wealth, he has limitless resources that have probably helped him do that. Based on the profile I've put together over the months, I'm all but certain he's already several steps ahead of us. We need to be careful to not...poke the beast." He gave Lachlan a knowing look, eyebrow raised.

"What are you getting at?"

"You can't just go into his office and accuse him of being a goddamn serial killer. We need ironclad evidence. Need to try to...catch him in the act."

"Catch him in the act?" Lachlan shot back with a

disbelieving laugh. "So... What? We're supposed to wait until October thirteenth and hope we know exactly when and where he plans on killing another innocent woman?"

"Without definitive evidence implicating him otherwise, I don't see any other option," Ethan argued as the sirens grew closer.

With each second that passed, my pulse increased. Hearing sirens wasn't an odd occurrence. Not in this city. There were areas of Atlanta that had pretty high crime rates. Still, I couldn't shake the premonition deep in my gut that something horrible was about to happen.

When the sirens came to a stop in front of my house, tires screeching, I knew it for certain.

"Mama!" Imogene shouted, darting down the stairs, eyes wide, panicked. "What's going on?"

"I don't know, baby." I wrapped her in my arms, a chill washing over me when an incessant knock sounded from my front door.

"Julia Prescott? Georgia State Patrol. I'm here to do a welfare check. It's important I speak with you immediately."

Heart in my throat, I swung my eyes to Lachlan's, both of us frozen in place.

"Please, ma'am. This is an emergency. I need to make sure both you and your daughter are okay."

Without waiting for me to give him permission, Lachlan strode toward the front door, while Ethan calmly collected his papers, returning them to his file. I kept my arm around Imogene, our steps slow as we walked into the foyer.

Lachlan pulled open the door, a large, Black man in a state trooper's uniform standing there. Recognition briefly flashed in his gaze when he saw Lachlan. Then he shifted his eyes to Imogene and me, a hint of relief within before his expression turned stoic once more.

Removing his hat, he squared his shoulders. "Ma'am, I'm Captain Patrick Dawson of the Georgia State Patrol."

I nodded slightly, not saying anything, fear snaking through me with every second that passed.

"I regret to be the one to inform you..." He glanced at Imogene before returning his gaze to mine, "but at approximately seven hundred hours this morning, the prison transport vehicle carrying Domenic Jaskulski crashed, resulting in several casualties."

I exhaled a tiny breath. "Nick's...dead?" Hope filled my voice, desperate to hear those words fall from his lips.

He slowly shook his head. "No, ma'am." He swallowed hard. "The prisoner... He wasn't found in the wreckage."

My breathing increased, heart racing as tremors

overtook my body. Imogene tightened her hold on me, tears filling her eyes.

"What are you saying?"

"Your ex-husband has escaped custody and his whereabouts are currently unknown."

I hope you enjoyed Provocation! Find out how it all ends in the final installment, OBSESSION!

Will Julia and Lachlan's love be strong enough to survive what's to come now that Nick's escaped custody? And what's his connection to all these recent deaths? Find out today!

https://www.tkleighauthor.com/temptationseries

I appreciate your help in spreading the word about my books. Please leave a review on your favorite book site.

OBSESSION

One week. No names. No expectations.

That was our agreement.

We were supposed to walk away after our time in Hawaii was over.

No matter what.

That was before...
Before I learned who she is.
Before I realized how interconnected our lives are.
Before I fell in love.

But our love isn't the stuff fairy tales are made of.

Demons lurk around every corner.

Good doesn't necessarily prevail over evil.

And the knight in shining armor may not save the day.

Not if Julia's murderous ex-husband has anything to do with it.

But she's never been the type of woman who needs a knight in shining armor to save the day.

She's the type of woman who will pick up her own sword and fight for what she believes in.

I just hope she's finally learned to believe in herself.

https://www.tkleighauthor.com/temptationseries

PLAYLIST

Found - Jacob Banks

Time Bomb - Dave Matthews Band

Beggin' - Maneskin

Unholy War - Jacob Banks

My Head & My Heart - Ava Max

Chasing Ghosts - Janelle Arthur

Just When I Thought - Jacob Banks

Tirer un trait - La Zarra

No Time to Die - Billie Ellish

Make it Rain - Sofia Karlberg

Beautiful night 4 a breakdown - Alaska Thunderfuck

Smile - Lily Kershaw

Love is Weird - Julia Michaels

I Of the Storm - Of Monsters and Men

Here's Your Perfect - Jamie Miller
I've Seen you Naked - Luch Stefano
The Wicked - Blues Saraceno
Cold Blood - Dave Not Dave

ACKNOWLEDGMENTS

Phew. Book three is in the books. And I certainly hope you enjoyed the ride.

One of the questions I get asked a lot as a writer is how I come up with my stories. Every author's different, but for me, it tends to be one scene in my mind that ends up being the basis for an entire story.

And for this series, it was the prison scene where Julia goes to visit her ex-husband for the first time.

While I love writing the love story between the hero and the heroine, I have to admit my favorite scenes to write in this series have been those with Nick. And there's much more to come in Obsession, the final book in this series!

Writing any book is quite a difficult task. And I

wouldn't be able to do it without the amazing team I have supporting me.

First and foremost, a huge thanks to my husband, Stan, and daughter, Harper Leigh. I couldn't do this without their support.

To my wonderful PA and alpha reader, Melissa Crump — Thank you so much for everything you do to keep me on task and making sure my author world runs smoothly. I couldn't do this without you.

To my fantastic beta readers — Lin, Sylvia, Stacy, and Vicky — thanks for reading and offering your feedback on this story. I'm so glad you've all fallen in love with this twisted story.

To my amazing editor — Kim Young. You're the only woman I'll ever trust with my babies. Thank you for treating them as if they were you're own.

To my girl, A.D. Justice. Thanks for always being there when I need advice, or just someone to bitch to, no questions asked.

To my admin team - Melissa, Vicky, Lea, Joelle. Thanks for keeping my reader group and Facebook page running. Love you ladies!

To my review team. Thanks for always taking the time to read and review my work. You are all amazing.

To my reader group. Thanks for being my super-fans and giving me a place to go when I need a break from writing.

And last but not least, a big thank you to YOU! My incredible readers. Whether this is your first T.K. book or you've read all of them, I'm so grateful you took a chance on my stories.

Stay tuned for the epic conclusion to Lachlan & Julia's story! What's going to happen now that Nick poses an even greater threat? Find out soon!

Love & Peace,

~ T.K.

ABOUT THE AUTHOR

T.K. Leigh is a *USA Today* Bestselling author of romance ranging from fun and flirty to sexy and suspenseful.

Originally from New England, she now resides just outside of Raleigh with her husband, beautiful daughter, rescued special needs dog, and three cats. When she's not writing, she can be found training for her next marathon or chasing her daughter around the house.

facebook.com/tkleighauthor

instagram.com/tkleigh

tiktok.com/@tkleigh

bookbub.com/authors/t-k-leigh

pinterest.com/tkleighauthor